Tl

AT THE DOOR

DANIEL HURST

www.danielhurstbooks.com

This is a work of fiction. Names, characters, businesses, places, events, locales, and incidents are either the products of the author's imagination or used in a fictitious manner. Any resemblance to actual persons, living or dead, or actual events is entirely coincidental.

PROLOGUE

It all started with a knock on the door.

If only I hadn't answered it, all of this might never have happened. Things certainly would have been different.

My perfect marriage wouldn't have been blown up.

My love for my husband wouldn't have been put to the test.

I certainly wouldn't have kicked him out.

But the past can't be changed. The fact remains that there was a knock at the door, and I went and answered it. That was the moment that my whole life changed. Such a simple, stupid moment. It should have been a completely forgettable thing, like taking out the bin bags or stubbing a toe on the corner of a doorframe.

A non-event. Tediously dull.

Just life.

But that knock at the door was so much more than that. It changed my life forever.

That's because it was the first time that I saw *her*.

The woman at the door changed everything. Nothing was ever the same again after she came calling. I hated her, yet in some twisted way, I also feel like I admired her. She was my complete opposite in almost every single way, and there was something fascinating in that.

There was something so simple about the way in which she broke my life apart.

I can’t stop thinking about her.

The woman at the door.

Why did you have to knock?

1

REBECCA

You can't beat a Saturday night. For my money, it's the best time of the week, and I'm sure I'm not alone in thinking that. Friday nights are great, don't get me wrong, but they are often laced with the fatigue that comes at the end of five full working days. Those evenings were much livelier when I was younger and sleep deprivation wasn't a factor in my life, but these days, I'm usually in bed at ten on a Friday. Maybe I shouldn't admit that. I've still got two years to go until my fortieth birthday, so I can hardly put my end-of-week weariness down to age. But it is what it is.

Fridays used to be the best.

But not anymore.

Sunday nights have been, are and always will be the worst night of the week. I think we can all agree on that. I've hated them since childhood when my parents would make me take a bath in preparation for a new school week, and I continue to hate them to this day as I get ready to go back to the office on Monday morning. Sunday nights are a dead zone. It's technically still the weekend, but you can't do any fun weekend things like getting drunk or having a night away in a hotel room in the country. That's because you have to be ready to go in the morning when the rat race commences again, and it's hard to do that if you're hungover or on the other side of the country from wherever your workplace might be.

I got drunk on a Sunday night once.

The Monday morning was so bad that I've never done it again.

Yes, there's no doubt in my mind that Saturday nights are the best night of the week. Fresh from a good night's sleep and a long lie-in, the first day of the weekend can be spent doing whatever I wish. Shopping for too many things. Eating too many calories. Drinking too many calories. Saturdays are fun, and it means that by the time the evening comes around, I'm feeling refreshed, revitalised and ready for romance. My husband and I have a Saturday night tradition. We order an Indian takeaway, we pick a good movie to watch, and we curl up on the sofa to spend an enjoyable few hours in each other's company. We don't judge the other one on how much curry we eat, and we don't fight over what film to watch. That's because we're far too comfortable with each other to care.

I've been married to Sam for three years, but we were together for eight years before that. That's a long time in anybody's book, well, anybody's except my parents. They have been together for fifty years and make jokes about how my relationship is still in its infancy. But eleven years is definitely a long time, and it explains why Sam and I are so settled with each other. Some people in their late thirties might want to spend their Saturday nights out on the town, clinging onto their last remnants of youth by drinking in dodgy pubs and trying to hold a conversation where the music is too loud to hold one. But not us. We're happy to hurtle headlong into middle age right here on our sofa with a masala and a couple of poppadoms in front of us and the smug and satisfied glow that comes with knowing that we are everything that the other person needs.

'Have you got any naan bread left?'

Sam's query is a simple one, and I reply with a simple answer.

'Yeah. Help yourself.'

I see Sam's hand reach out for the large piece of bread sitting by my plate and smile, not because he is taking my food but because I knew he would. He does this every week. He starts by telling me that he is cutting down on carbs, so he will not be ordering any naan from the takeaway. I ask him if he is sure because I know how much he likes to dip the bread in his curry sauce when he gets going. But he always insists that he doesn't want one. Fast-forward to an hour later when the food has arrived, and he's looking at me and my naan forlornly before the question comes.

He knows I always have some left for him.

That's because I know he is always going to ask.

The food has been exceptionally good tonight, even though we always order from the same place. Maybe they have a new chef, or perhaps the cooks were in a slightly better mood this evening and made more of an effort. Whatever the reason, I'm feeling very pleased with my meal, even if I have just lost a chunk of it to my husband.

The film we chose to watch is not bad either. It's a comedy about a woman trying to adjust to becoming a mum. I'm finding it funny, although maybe that's because I don't have children of my own. That means I can laugh at how terrifying it all is for somebody else. I'm surprised Sam agreed to watch this movie because I was sure that he was going to ask me to pick something else, but he's been laughing away a couple of times at some of the jokes too.

Or at least he has when his mouth hasn't been full of my naan bread.

All in all, it's a very normal Saturday night. A quick check on the time tells me that it has only just gone eight, which means there are still a few more hours of the evening to enjoy yet. Maybe there will be time for another movie after this one, or maybe Sam and I will head into the bedroom early and add a little more spice to our evening to go along with the curry.

We should probably have sex tonight. It's been over a week, and I know he'll be thinking about it. I'm thinking about it too, but I could easily go another night, especially now I've just eaten my bodyweight in Indian food. But I'll see how I'm feeling after the film. Maybe I'll come onto him when we get in bed. Or maybe I'll just do it right here on the sofa.

It is Saturday night, after all.

But any plans we have are thrown into mild disarray by the sudden knocking at the door.

'Who's that at this time?' Sam asks with a mouthful of naan bread.

'I don't know. I'm not expecting anybody. Are you?'

'No. Is it another one of your packages?'

'I don't think so. I haven't ordered anything recently.'

I usually take delivery of at least three or four things a week from my favourite online stores, keeping the local delivery drivers busy, as well as keeping my husband irritated at all the cardboard boxes piling up in the hallway. But I definitely haven't ordered anything for a while, so it can't be that. And neither of us are expecting a friend or family member to call around at this time either.

So who is it?

'I'll go,' Sam says, putting down his knife and fork and trying to swallow down a bit of naan bread before he stands. But I've already finished eating, so I decide to take this one.

'It's okay, love. I've got it.'

I get up from the sofa and head for the living room door, leaving behind the food and drinks, as well as the movie that still has a while to run.

'Do you want me to pause it?' Sam asks helpfully, but I shake my head.

'It's fine. I'll be back in a second.'

I leave the room and enter the hallway, thinking that whoever it is at the door will have the wrong address. It's probably a takeaway driver getting mixed up on our street. It happens every now and again because of the way the houses are numbered around here. The numbers are all over the place as if they were assigned by a sulky school kid who hated Maths and just wanted to get it over with as quickly as possible. We're next to number six, which means we should either be four or eight. But we're not.

We're fourteen.

Yeah, it's messed up.

I reach the front door and take off the latch, which didn't really need to be on until we went to bed, but I like to put it on early if we're staying in because it makes me feel safer and saves me a job later.

God, I am getting old, aren't I?

With the latch off, I just need to turn the handle. As I do, the door swings open and I get a good look at the person standing on the doorstep.

But they're not what I was expecting. Instead of an overweight male delivery driver clutching a bag of someone else's food, I see a blonde woman wearing a smart black coat. Her red lipstick matches her red fingernails, and it looks as if she is ready for a night out. If she is then she is definitely in the wrong place. But before I can say anything, she speaks first.

'Are you Rebecca Andrews?' she asks me.

'Yes.'

'The wife of Sam Andrews?'

'That's right. Who are you?'

'I'm the woman he slept with last month. I'm guessing that he didn't tell you about me.'

2

SAM

I can feel the draught from the open front door all the way in here. I'm not sure who it is out there, but I'm hoping Rebecca can get rid of them quickly so we can go back to enjoying our night. I know she said that she didn't want me to pause the movie for her, but I've done it anyway. It's partly because I don't want her to miss anything while she is out of the room, but mainly it's because she'll spend the rest of the film asking me what's happening if I don't. It's just easier if I pause it so that we can pick up where we left off when she returns.

But she isn't back yet, and the chilly air from outside is still seeping into our house.

I think about getting off the sofa and going to see who it is at the door, but that would require me moving, and that's easier said than done after all the food I've eaten tonight. I've not finished yet though thanks to Rebecca kindly giving me her leftover naan bread, and I'm very much looking forward to using it to mop up the last of my curry sauce. But I can't do that if I'm out in the hallway, so I stay where I am and keep eating.

I do feel slightly guilty for eating this bread when I had made the vow to myself to give up carbs for a while. It's a vow I have made several times in the past, and I am yet to stick to it. I really thought tonight would be the night when I exercised some restraint and stayed away from the dreaded bread, but alas, here I am again, scoffing down the extra calories as if it's my last meal on Earth.

It's not that I'm overweight and really need to lose a few pounds or anything. It's just that I know I will feel better within myself if I curb my carb consumption. After all, I'm not eighteen anymore. I'm thirty-eight now, and the pounds are slowly starting to pile on, which means I have to do something if I don't want to be reasonably rotund by the time I hit forty. There's not much one can do about getting older but keeping in shape is definitely within my control, so I do need to make the effort.

Starting tomorrow, of course.

I finish off my delightful meal, ensuring that there isn't a scrap of food left in any of the silver trays that were dropped off here by a polite Indian man an hour ago, before taking a deep breath and sinking back into the sofa. I feel like a whale, and right now, I probably look like one too. My stomach is bloated, thanks to the curry and naan, although the two pints of lager that I washed it all down with haven't helped there either. If I had my way, I wouldn't move now until bedtime, which will probably be when this movie finishes. It won't be a late night, and I do like the idea of getting into bed early with Rebecca and seeing where the mood takes us, but then again, I'm not exactly feeling like a Casanova with a full curry inside of me. Hopefully, my stomach will go down, and I'll be feeling a little more energetic when the film finishes. But the pause symbol is still showing on the TV screen, which means the film won't be finishing anytime soon. That's because Rebecca is still not back yet from answering the door.

What is taking her so long?

I decide to go and investigate, but I'm one of the few talented men that can do two things at once, so I pick up our dirty plates as I go, planning on dumping them in the kitchen after I've checked on my wife in the hallway.

Carrying the plates to the door, I notice that Rebecca has left some of her rice. Unlike me, she is able to exercise some level of control around carbohydrates. I'd ask her for some tips if I knew she wouldn't laugh at me.

Leaving the room, I enter the hallway, and that's when I hear Rebecca calling out of the open doorway.

'Wait! Come back!' she cries, although I'm not sure who she is talking to because I can't see the other person. It looks like they have already left, but I walk towards the door to see if I can get a glimpse of them anyway. But just before I reach the door, Rebecca turns and sees me standing there holding the plates with a confused expression on my face. But it's not my expression that is the problem.

It's hers.

She looks distressed.

'Who was it?' I ask, wishing I could put the plates down somewhere but feeling like this is more important at the minute.

But Rebecca doesn't answer me. Instead, she just glares at me, and that's when I notice that she has tears in her eyes.

'Rebecca. What's happened?' I ask, and this time, I decide to do something about the plates so that I can make sure she is alright.

I put them on the bottom step of the staircase before reaching out for my wife with my now-empty hands, but she moves away from me, which is very unlike her.

'What's happened?' I ask again, and I've lost count of how many questions that is now since I came out here. But I know how many times she has answered me.

Zero.

'Rebecca?'

'Get away from me.'

Her response is shocking both in its content and delivery. She spoke the words in such a harsh manner as if she really meant it.

'Will you tell me what's going on?' I plead, feeling the cold air blowing in from the open doorway and wondering if Rebecca can feel it too. She must do. So why isn't she closing the door?

Why does she look like she wants to run out of it?

'Rebecca. Please!'

I sound more desperate now, but that's only because I am feeling it. I have never seen my wife like this before. She looks like she hates me, but that doesn't make any sense. Two minutes ago, we were having a great Saturday night with a takeaway and a film. One knock at the door and all that has changed.

Who the hell was it?

'Will you at least close the door? It's freezing,' I say, hoping that a bit of common sense might be the thing to do the trick and get us to be more communicative with each other again. But it seems that my wife's mood towards me is even colder than the weather outside, and she ignores my request, instead remaining at a safe distance from me in the open doorway.

'I don't know what to say,' I confess, throwing up my hands in despair. 'If you don't tell me what this is about then how I can help?'

'Who was she?' Rebecca asks, and the question catches me off guard, not just because I wasn't expecting her to speak.

'Who?'

'The woman that just turned up on my doorstep.'

'What woman?'

I try to look past Rebecca and out onto the street to see who she might be talking about, but it's too dark out there, and I can't see anybody.

'There was a woman here just now. She said she knew you.'

'What was her name?'

'I don't know. She didn't tell me.'

'Then how am I supposed to know who it is?'

'I think you know.'

That last comment from my wife is said with a hint of menace, and I don't like it at all. I genuinely have no idea who she is talking about, but I know that I can't keep saying that because it will only make her angrier. But what else can I say?

'Can you come back in and close the door so we can talk?' I suggest. But that doesn't work either.

'Not until you tell me if it's true.'

'If what's true?'

'Did you have an affair?'

Of all the surprising things that have happened, starting with the knock at the door a few minutes ago, that is the one that gets me the most.

'An affair? What are you talking about?'

'She said she slept with you last month?'

'What? Who did?'

'The woman!'

Rebecca is on the verge of tears, and I hate it, mainly because I have no idea how to make her feel better.

'I don't know what has happened, but I've not slept with anybody,' I say, shaking my head. 'Are you sure she had the right house?'

'Yes, I'm sure!' Rebecca hisses back. 'She knew our names!'

'Okay, okay, calm down,' I say before reaching out for my wife again, but she just bats my hand away as if it's a fly on a hot summer's day.

'Don't tell me to calm down! How would you feel if somebody turned up and said I'd slept with somebody else.'

'But it's not true!'

'Prove it!'

‘How can I do that? I don’t even know who this bloody woman is!’

I must have a point because Rebecca doesn’t have a comeback for me right away. Instead, she closes the door, and at first, I feel relieved because I think she is calming down. But I’m wrong.

She is just getting started.

3

REBECCA

It's been five minutes since my perfect Saturday night was interrupted by a knock at the door. It's been four minutes since a female stranger told me that my husband had strayed. And it's been one minute since I demanded that Sam tell me the truth about what has happened.

But so far, I have no answers.

So far, my husband is denying it all.

'Rebecca, I don't know what to tell you other than the truth, which is that I have no idea who this woman could be and why she would say such a thing!'

I glare at Sam, trying to read him, which was always something that I felt I could do. But now I'm not so sure.

Maybe I don't know him as well as I thought I did.

Maybe I never knew him at all.

I storm past him and go back into our living room, where the empty takeaway boxes on the table are evidence of the fact that this was once an innocent evening. I also notice that Sam has paused the movie for me, which I would have thought of as considerate a few minutes ago but not any more now that I have more important things to think about.

'Rebecca, will you just listen to me?'

Sam has followed me in here, as I knew he would, and I was planning on taking a seat to have the rest of this conversation, but now that I'm standing by the sofa, I realise that I'm far too anxious to sit. Instead, I keep pacing, and it's Sam's turn to stand in the doorway and look at me with a worried expression on his face.

'She said last month. Where did you go last month?'

I say the question out loud, but it's as much for me to answer as it is for Sam. I'm racking my brains trying to recall if my husband had a night away from me a month ago, but I can't think of anything, and it turns out that Sam can't either.

'I didn't go anywhere!' he tells me, and despite my best efforts, I can't think of a time when he stayed away overnight. But then I realise that doesn't mean he is innocent. Who said anything about it being a sordid night in a seedy hotel? He could very easily have cheated on me during the day.

Maybe at his office. Maybe at her house.

Maybe here.

'Why would somebody say this if it wasn't true?' I ask him as I continue to walk around the room erratically. I'm going to wear a hole in this patch of carpet if I'm not careful, but I'm not going to be able to stand still until my heart rate has come down, and that won't happen until I get to the bottom of this.

'I have no idea, but it isn't true. I swear.'

'I want to believe you.'

'Then believe me!'

'But why would she say it? Why would she turn up here? How does she know my name, and how does she know where we live?'

The volume of my voice was increasing with each question that I asked of my husband, and he perhaps wisely waits a second before answering me so that I can simmer down again.

'Look, I don't know who this woman is and why she said those things. But you're right. If she knows who we are and where we live, I guess I must know her. I just need to figure out who it is and why she would say such a thing.'

That all sounds very logical, and Sam said it in a way that almost made me think that this is just a puzzle that needs to be solved, like a game of Sudoku on a train or a Rubik's cube on Christmas morning. But it's not a puzzle. It's so much more than that.

It's our relationship.

My anger has subsided a little now, and that is how I'm able to finally stop pacing around and take a seat on the sofa. Sam seems relieved by that and comes to join me, sitting down beside me, although he opts not to try and take my hand again until he knows for sure that I'm not going to reject him for a second time.

'I don't know what to do,' I confess, shaking my head and feeling my eyes watering. 'I can't believe this has happened.'

'Neither can I. But it's not true, Bec. I swear to God it's not true.'

Sam sometimes calls me Bec, usually when he wants something or is trying to cheer me up. I guess in this case it is the latter, although it could be both. I guess he wants me to believe him.

But do I?

I wipe my eyes and take a deep breath as Sam gets up from the sofa and goes in search of a box of tissues. While he's gone, I think about the man I married and everything I know about him because that is an important thing to do now. It's important because it will be how I decide whether I believe him or not.

What do I know about him? I know that he is extremely caring, a trait he demonstrated when we first met after he gave up his seat for me on the tube one busy morning in London. I know that he is charming, a trait he proved when he chatted to me for the remainder of that tube journey before he asked me out for a drink later that week. And I know that he is generous, which he proved when he paid for not just one drink on that first date but several of them, as well as the meal we went on for our second date.

I know him to be a funny man, and he has made me laugh every day that I have been with him and never more so than during his speech on our wedding day. I know him to be a hardworking man, and he regularly puts in long days at the office where he works as a project consultant. And I know that he is honest because I have never caught him in a lie before and the only time that he kept something from me was when he had organised a surprise for Valentine's Day last year.

Perhaps most importantly, I know that he is loyal, a quality he has demonstrated with his dedication to his employers, his support of his favourite football team, his availability to friends and family, and best of all, to me.

He adores me. He worships me.

He loves me.

So with all that I know about him, what is the verdict? Do I believe him, or do I believe that woman at the door?

I have my answer when he walks back into the room carrying a box of tissues for me.

See, there's that caring side.

'Here you go,' he says as he re-takes his seat next to me and hands me the box.

I thank him and pull out a couple of tissues before wiping my eyes and dabbing at my nose. I hardly ever get emotional, not because I'm cold-hearted but because I'm usually able to stay in control and look at things logically. That's one of my traits, which is why I have ended up working as an engineer for a small construction company. It's also why I was able to process things and move on when a specialist told me that I wasn't able to have children. I did shed some tears that day, but I was able to pull myself together fairly quickly thanks to the way my brain works. It sees a problem and it tries to solve it. This might be a very unexpected problem that I have to try and solve, but it doesn't mean that I can't do it.

Or rather, it doesn't mean that *we* can't do it.

'I believe you,' I say to Sam, reaching out for his hand and giving it a squeeze.

He looks relieved to hear me say it, but I'm afraid it's not going to be that simple.

'We need to find out who that woman was,' I tell him, fixing him with a determined stare. 'I need to know who she is. Otherwise, it'll be impossible to forget about it.'

Sam nods his head and tells me that he understands. But he swears to me again that he has done nothing wrong and that he loves me. I smile and tell him that I know, then we hug.

The film is still on pause in the background, and until we find out who that mystery woman was, I feel like our relationship is on pause too.

4

SAM

The first thing that I needed to do was calm my wife down and make her believe me when I said that I had done nothing wrong with that woman. The second thing to do is figure out who the hell that woman was, and all I have to go on is what Rebecca can tell me about her.

'What did she look like? Was she young? Old?'

'I think she was around our age.'

'What colour hair did she have?'

'Blonde.'

'Blonde…' I repeat, mentally visualising all the blonde women that I have known in my life. But there's been a few, although none of them who I could imagine would turn up on my doorstep and make false accusations.

'Was she tall or short?' I ask, although that's probably not going to help me narrow it down much because of all the women I do know, none of them are tall.

'I don't know. I didn't pay much attention to her looks. I was more concerned with what she was telling me.'

I think about that because it seems that it might be my best lead. What did the woman tell Rebecca? She said that I slept with her a month ago. The clue must be in the timeframe.

What exactly was I doing a month ago?

'Hang on a minute,' I say, getting up off the sofa and going out into the hallway to where my work satchel is sitting near the bottom of the stairs. As I pick it up, I realise that the two dirty plates are still on the bottom step of the staircase and I really should put them in the kitchen, but this is more important, so I leave them and return to Rebecca in the living room.

Sitting down beside her again, I go into my satchel and take out my work diary from the inner compartment. I'm hoping that this will provide the answers as to what I was doing a month ago, and I thumb through the pages of it quickly to go back to the relevant dates.

It's the 7th of February today, so I'm going back to early January, that frigid time of year when everybody in England is fed up with the cold weather and full from overindulging at Christmas, yet still facing a few more months of bleak winter and valiantly having a crack at their New Year's resolutions. By this present date, most people will have given up on those resolutions, but back then, when the year was still young, there would have been hope, and it's hope that keeps me turning these pages in search of an answer as to who the woman at the door really was.

I decide to start from January 4th because that was the first working day back in the office after the festive period, and I see the various meetings that I had scribbled into this diary that took place back then. There was a project design meeting that afternoon, as well as a conference call on the 5th but nothing unusual or anything that could help me figure out what this woman could have been referring to. A check on the 6th, 7th and 8th yields no returns either, and then it was the weekend, which I recall spending with Rebecca re-decorating the spare bedroom. We always like to get the house jobs done in winter so that we are free to enjoy the summer, and January had been no different. The spare bedroom was now looking good, and it was all thanks to the work that my wife and I did in early January.

That was a month ago.

So what the hell is this woman talking about?

'I didn't go anywhere but the office a month ago,' I tell Rebecca as I shake my head and continue to turn the pages of my diary.

'Could it be someone from work?' she asks me. 'That could be how they know who I am and where you live.'

'But why would somebody from my office say these things? It doesn't make any sense.'

Rebecca continues watching me search my diary, but I give up after I've been through the whole month and not found a single thing that says I stayed away for a night or deviated from my usual schedule. I know my wife must be having a hard time trusting me, but she has to understand that I'm also having a hard time trying to figure this out. I want answers, and I want them because that will be the only way that I can be sure that Rebecca trusts me again. While there is a lingering doubt, she will always have the thought in her head about the man I might really be.

Closing my diary, I put it back into my satchel and run my fingers along my chin as I think. I'm aware that I'm doing it, and I could stop, but I find myself rubbing my chin more and more these days when I have something tricky to ponder. My father did the same thing and I used to tease him about it, never thinking that I would one day end up exhibiting the exact same mannerism, but here I am, behaving just like him. I seem to be turning into my old man more and more as I get older, although there is one area where I will never follow in his footsteps.

I will never stray and break the heart of the woman I married.

I was fourteen when I came home from school to find my mother in tears and her best friend by her side offering support. I didn't know what had happened until Mum told me later that night when she came into my room and sat down on my bed. She said that my father had found somebody else and that he wouldn't be living with us anymore. It was a shock, and I ended up crying just as much as my mum, but that didn't change the fact that my parents' once happy marriage had come to an end. I ignored Dad for a while after that but eventually gave him a chance to make things up to me when he bought me tickets to see my favourite football team in the cup final. I felt like I was betraying Mum by seeing him again, but she was okay with it, and she made it clear that he was the one who had done the wrong thing, not me. Dad and I were never as close after that as we were before, but he was still very much a part of my life, and I was glad he came to my wedding to Rebecca. I was glad that he didn't bring his new wife because Mum was there, and that would have been upsetting. But that experience showed me the damage that can be caused when one person breaks their word to another and ruins a relationship, which is why adultery is one sin you will never catch me committing. Yet that is the sin I have been accused of tonight, and what is even more infuriating than being accused of doing something that I didn't do is not knowing who my accuser is.

I continue to think about the women in my life and who I might know who could have been the one to call at my home this evening. There are a few blonde women in my friendship group, but Rebecca knows them, so she would have recognised them if they came here. There's a blonde woman in my office, but she's in her fifties, and Rebecca believed her to be of a similar age to us. And there are several blonde women at my gym, but I have never spoken to any of them, and they shouldn't know where I live, who I'm married to or have any reason to make up a lie about me.

So with all that considered, who am I left with?

Nobody. I don't have the slightest idea who this person could be, and that is very troubling to me. It's troubling because I don't know why she decided to come here tonight.

It's also troubling because I don't know if she is planning on coming back.

5

THE WOMAN

I have just paid a visit to Sam and Rebecca's house and dropped the bombshell on their doorstep before turning and walking away into the night. I expect they are now having an interesting conversation in which all manner of topics will be on the table.

Trust. Loyalty.

Lies.

I'd love to be a fly on the wall in that house, eavesdropping on their discussion and hearing what Rebecca has to say to her husband, as well as all the ways in which he tries to defend himself. But I couldn't hang around for too long. My visit will have had more of an impact if I just said what I needed to say and left.

I want to cause maximum shock and maximum confusion.

I imagine that it is mission accomplished.

The sound of my high heels on concrete is the only noise on this quiet road now as I make my way towards my car, which I parked a couple of streets over from where Sam lives. I didn't want either him or his wife to see the number plate of my vehicle as that would have been a possible way for them to try and find out who I was if they shared that information with the police, although I'm not sure how interested the police would have been in looking for me. After all, there has been no crime committed here tonight. I'm just a woman who knocked on a door and said a few words. I didn't swear or shout. I kept calm, said my piece and I didn't stay for a minute longer than I needed to.

In the eyes of the law, there is nothing wrong with saying what I did.

But in the eyes of a happy marriage, there is a lot wrong with it.

Telling a woman that I slept with her husband is the kind of thing that won't be forgotten easily by the married couple, and their discussion of my claim is sure to put their relationship to the test. But of course, that's exactly what I want. The way I see it, Rebecca and Sam are a pillar of stone, and I am a chisel. They are strong while I am crafty. They appear sturdy, but I can find a weakness.

They might seem unbreakable, but I can cause them to crack.

There is no doubt that there is a crack in their relationship now. How big that crack is remains to be seen, but like any good craftsman with his trusty tool, I will keep chipping away until I break through and get what I need.

I will turn those cracks into deep fissures.

I had no idea which one of the pair would answer the door when I knocked on it this evening, but I was prepared for either eventuality. If it had been Sam, I had another script to say, and it would have been very different to the one I ended up using on Rebecca. But I'm glad it was her that I spoke to.

I find this always works best when it's the wife who answers the door.

Reaching my vehicle, I make a quick check behind me to make sure that I haven't been followed before opening the door and getting in behind the wheel. Taking off my heels, I replace them with the trainers that I had waiting for me on the passenger seat, and my aching feet thank me for the change. I didn't have to wear heels for the visit tonight, but I feel that they are more effective for what I was aiming to do. Rebecca would have been intimidated by me no matter what I was wearing after what I just said to her, but heels will have more impact than trainers, that's for sure.

I want her to think that I'm a maneater, not a marathon runner.

With my comfy trainers back on, I'm in a better state to drive, so I start the engine and put my car into motion. It's a short drive back to where I am staying tonight, and I'm already looking forward to getting changed and having a warm shower before relaxing on the bed and finding something good to watch on the TV. But I'll find it hard to concentrate on anything else this evening other than Rebecca and Sam and what they are saying about me right now.

Sam will be saying that I was lying but isn't that what every man would say if their wife thought they had been cheating? He will also be saying that he has no idea who I am. Again, what else could he say? He could hardly admit to anything that might see him kicked out of the house, could he?

Rebecca will be saying that I seemed assured and sincere when I spoke, or at least I hope she will be because I did try my best to get across how seriously I took this whole situation. I didn't smile, or frown, or laugh. I just told her what she needed to hear and left her to decide what to do next.

She might hate me. She might believe me. Or she might be taking Sam's side.

But one thing is for sure.

She won't be able to forget me.

That's the main thing. That's all that tonight was really about. Like that first blow from the chisel on the stone pillar. It won't bring the whole thing down. But it is a start. It will let the pillar know that it is in for a war, and that's what Rebecca and Sam are in for now.

A war.

Tonight was just the opening battle, and I won that.

I have no doubt that I am going to win the war too.

Why wouldn't I?

I haven't lost one yet.

6

REBECCA

What was I saying about Saturday nights being the best nights of the week? This one has been terrible, easily the worst night of my marriage so far, but as bad as it's been, it's not over yet. That's because I can't go to sleep until I have a better understanding of what happened here a couple of hours ago with that woman at the door.

I'm in bed, but I'm sitting up and waiting for Sam to finish what he is doing in the bathroom so that we can talk. We've had a little break from analysing the upsetting incident, although only verbally. Mentally, the questions are still running amok in my head, and I imagine they will be for quite some time.

There wasn't much I could do to forget about it. Clearing away the dirty dishes after the takeaway didn't help. Nor was I in the mood to continue watching the film, which meant we turned the television off; that paused movie now likely to go unfinished forever because watching the rest of it at a later date will only remind me of this night again. I've tried browsing social media because that's usually good for a distraction, but it only ended up making me feel worse, as social media has a tendency to do. That's because I saw plenty of photos and statuses from married friends, many of whom were out for a meal tonight or on holiday somewhere having a great time, looking like they were very much in love without a care in the world. Normally, I would have been liking all those photos and adding a few positive comments beneath them, but not tonight. All those status updates did tonight were remind me that my relationship is far from perfect.

Unlike those happy people online, I do have a care in the world.

I hear the toilet flush in the bathroom and prepare myself for Sam's arrival back into the bedroom, where we will once again pick up the conversation and try to get to the bottom of what went on here tonight. As I decided earlier, I believe my husband and will continue to trust him despite what has happened. I have to do so because it's his word over the word of a complete stranger who offered no evidence to back up her claims, so my husband's word carries far more weight.

Sam has already brought up the possibility of it being somebody who was playing a prank. Perhaps the woman had enjoyed one too many drinks today and decided to have a little 'fun' on her way home. Maybe a friend dared her to do it, and she might have been hidden out of sight somewhere watching on and getting a good kick out of it. That is one of several possibilities, and it's the one that I would like to be the truth, although it doesn't explain how the woman knew our names. If it's a prank, I can handle it because it means that my husband has not strayed and that he is still the loyal and loving man whom I married. But the problem if it is a prank is that the perpetrator of it is hardly likely to come back again and let me know that was the case. Therefore, I'll never totally be sure.

There will always be a doubt at the back of my mind.

The toilet door unlocks, and I watch the bedroom doorway for Sam to appear in it. When he does, he has something else to say to me to presumably try and put my mind at ease.

'Look, I know this has been a horrible night, but the more I think about it, the more it has to be a prank. The problem is, that would mean it was set up by somebody who knew both of our names, and I'm not sure who would want to do that to us.'

I shake my head, mainly because I have no idea of who that could be either but also because I still can't believe this has happened. If it is some kind of a joke, it's a sick one. Who has the right to go around and potentially blow up people's marriages just for a cheap thrill? The initial anger I had for my husband is now directed at the person or persons who had the idea to do this, and I wish I could get a hold of that damn woman and give her a slap for coming to my door and telling lies. But I can't. She walked away, and I was too stunned to go after her. If only I had chased her down the street, maybe I could have found out what all of this was about. Instead, I'm left sitting here in my bed, looking at my husband with a slightly different perspective.

No matter how much I tell myself that I trust him and believe his side of the story, which is that there is no story, there is still that little voice telling me that the woman was speaking the truth and she was trying to help me by revealing the man I am really married to. But I don't want to believe that, so I won't. I'm an adult, and I can believe what I want.

Therefore, I believe that my husband has been, is and always will be faithful to me.

'I really wish you'd let me answer the door,' Sam says as he sits on his side of the bed and pulls off his socks. 'If only I'd have seen her.'

'It doesn't matter. Let's just go to sleep,' I say, shuffling down in the bed until my head is on the pillow. But if only it was that easy. I'm going to be wide awake all night, and I know it.

I'm going to be thinking about that woman and my husband together.

As if reading my mind, Sam leans over and gives me a kiss on the head before telling me to try and not think about it anymore. I give him a weak smile before nodding my head and rolling over so that my back is turned to him. I'm not being purposefully distant. I just need to think logically, and I can't do that by looking at him because there is too much emotion there.

The bed shakes as Sam joins me under the duvet, and there is a little rummaging on his side before the bedside lamp goes off and we are plunged into darkness. I feel his arm go around my waist, a move that would normally make me smile and feel incredibly loved, but tonight, it makes me feel sick.

That's because it's almost a reminder of what I stand to lose if this turns out to be true.

I couldn't stay with him if he has cheated on me. I could try, but it wouldn't work. I know what I'm like, and I'd never be able to get that thought of the other woman out of my head. The thing is, Sam knows this because I've told him as much before. Not in a serious or firm way, just when we have been joking around about that kind of thing. But it always ends with Sam saying the same thing. He tells me that he would never be unfaithful because he saw what his father did to his mother and how much pain it caused. That always added an extra buffer to the trust I had for my husband as if his experiences meant there was even less of a chance he would do anything. But as I lie here now in the dark, the paranoid thoughts begin to come, as they have a nasty habit of doing when all is quiet at the end of the day. They are the thoughts that say if Sam's old man could cheat, so could he. Maybe it's in the genes.

Like father, like son.

I shake my head as if to send the horrible thoughts scurrying back to whichever dark hole they came out of, and to make sure the thoughts don't return, I roll over and face my husband. Even though we can't see each other in this light, I know our faces are only a few inches apart. I can feel his breath on my cheeks, and while sometimes that is annoying when I'm trying to sleep, tonight I tell myself that it is reassuring.

It's my bed he is in. Not hers.

He is here with me. He is mine.

He is a good man. I have nothing to worry about.

Nothing at all.

7

SAM

I am a good man. I don't know what I did to deserve a woman coming to my house and making false accusations, but I can rest easy in the end because my conscience is clear. That must have been how I was able to fall asleep relatively quickly last night. Now it's morning, and the sunlight streaming through the curtains over the window makes everything seem much better than it did a few hours ago when everything was dark, including my wife's mood.

I usually hate that so much light comes through our bedroom curtains because it wakes me up on sunny mornings, and I have been meaning to get a black-out blind to put over the window. But like many things in my life, including charity work and skiing holidays, I never seem to get around to doing it. That could be why I have woken up now. It's too bright here.

Or maybe it's just because I have that mysterious woman on my mind again.

Just before I drifted off to sleep, I had an idea, and it's one that I am going to explore today. It was as I was cursing my bad luck for not knowing what this woman looked like when I remembered that our neighbour, Steve, has a camera on his driveway. That means it is possible that it captured footage of the woman arriving and leaving my house last night, and if so, there is potentially a way for me to see what she looks like and see if I can place her from anywhere. I'll have to ask Steve, of course, but I can do that. But I will have to make up a cover story because I can hardly tell him the truth, which is that I'm trying to find the woman who accused me of cheating on my wife. I'm not sure that would go down well. It definitely wouldn't go down well if Steve's wife got wind of it. I'll just have to make up something about someone playing pranks at our door last night and a need to check if any kids were hanging around. He'll buy that.

I'm eager to get up and get on with my plan, but Rebecca is still asleep, and I don't want to disturb her, so I lie still and occupy myself with my mobile phone. That's when I have the idea of scrolling through my friends online and making a shortlist of all the blonde women I have on there. I could show them to my wife to see if she identifies any of them as the woman at the door last night. It's highly unlikely that she would. These people are supposed to be friends of mine, not foes, but it might be worth a shot, and at least it will show her that I am serious about trying to get to the bottom of this. I think the worst thing I could do when it comes to this situation is to try and sweep it under the rug because that might look suspicious. Instead, I'm going to tackle it head-on and hopefully get to the bottom of it.

If somebody was playing a game with us then they are going to wish that they hadn't.

Tapping my thumb on the app that I do all my social networking on, I go to my list of friends and start scrolling, looking out for any and all blondes on there. I feel like I'm some seedy guy hunting around for a specific type of woman on a seedy website, but my intentions are pure.

I just want to know who that bloody woman was at the door.

It doesn't take long for me to find a few blondes, and I screenshot their images for later use. It seems silly to do this because many of these women are either good friends or have been in my real-world life for years, but I can't discriminate. I don't have much to go off other than hair colour, so that is what I will work on.

After ten minutes of scrolling and screenshotting, I'm a little surprised at how many blonde women I have on my friends list. It's not exactly a harem, but there's a few. Five more minutes go by before I reach the bottom of the list and feel satisfied that I have done all I can there. I will wait for Rebecca to wake up and then show her the images if she wants to see them, and perhaps we get lucky and find the culprit. Or maybe it would be unlucky because if the woman is on my friends list, she is no longer a friend of mine.

Returning my phone to the bedside table, I long to stand up and stretch out, but Rebecca seems so peaceful beside me that I don't want to cause her to stir. I'm just glad she is sleeping because I had been worried that she would be up all night thinking about all sorts of things regarding that damn woman. But the gentle sounds of her soft snoring let me know that she must have enough peace of mind to get some rest, and I'm happy for her to stay that way for as long as possible.

Besides, it's Sunday morning, and if a person can't have a lie-in on a Sunday morning, when can they?

I've always liked Sundays, sometimes more than Saturdays. Some people don't like them because it's the day before another working week begins, but that doesn't bother me. Unlike most people, I don't hate my job and spend half the weekend dreading going back to it. I know Rebecca dislikes Sunday nights with a passion and is very much a Saturday girl, but I'm a Sunday guy all the way. Newspapers in the morning, a good roast dinner in a pub in the afternoon, and an entertaining couple of episodes of a British boxset in the evening. It's hard to beat that.

Let's just hope today goes better than yesterday.

It's a couple of minutes later when I feel Rebecca moving beside me in the bed, and I look over to see her opening her eyes and squinting in the bright light penetrating that pathetic excuse for a curtain.

Maybe today will be the day when I go and buy that black-out blind.

Or maybe not.

As Rebecca's eyesight adjusts, I smile at her, and she gives me a smile back, although it's not as warm as it usually is. Or maybe I'm just reading too much into it. She's just woken up, after all. I need to give her a chance. But to make sure that things really are still okay between us, I reach out an arm and put it over her waist, letting her know that she is to snuggle in closer to me, and she takes the invitation, which is a good sign. As we kiss, I feel like everything is okay, and I'm almost tempted not to bring up the screenshots on my phone for her to look at. But then she speaks, and it lets me know that the awkward situation last night is still very much on her mind.

'I dreamt about giving that woman a slap,' she says, and I laugh when I realise that she is joking.

'I wish I'd seen her so I could visualise that too. She definitely deserves it.'

'I'm not sure that a man beating up a woman is okay, even in a dream,' Rebecca replies, and she might have a point.

'Fair enough,' I say before reaching over and picking up my phone from the bedside table.

'I've had a couple of ideas while you were sleeping about possibly figuring out who this woman might be,' I say before running her through my two ideas which consist of the screenshots and asking Steve for a look at his camera footage.

She tells me that they're both worth a shot, so I give her my phone, and she starts looking at the images.

I let her go through them in silence so as not to distract her, but it seems we have no luck.

'No, it's not any of them,' she tells me after a couple of minutes, and I feel disappointed, although this was hardly a fool-proof plan.

'Oh well, it was worth a try,' I say, taking back my phone. 'I'll get dressed and call around at Steve's later then.'

'Can I come?' she asks me, and I'm a little surprised that she wants to considering that I know she doesn't like Steve, or rather, she doesn't like his attitude towards women. It's not that Steve is a total chauvinist, but he has made some dodgy remarks over the years about the fairer sex, whether it's been at neighbourhood barbecues or sometimes just when we pass on our driveways. But if Rebecca wants to come with me then I guess she can.

'Sure,' I say with a shrug. 'Let's go do some detective work.'

8

REBECCA

I tuck my hair behind my ears and fiddle with the neckline on my blouse as Sam and I wait for Steve or his wife to come and answer the front door. I'm not sure why I feel nervous about going into this house, but it might have something to do with the fact that I know Steve can be a bit of a male chauvinist, so I guess I feel like he is going to judge me and my appearance as soon as he sees me. But I shouldn't care what he thinks. If he has a problem with women then it is his problem, not mine.

I'm just here to check his CCTV footage with my husband to see if we can spot the woman who came to our door last night.

I see movement through the frosted glass window of our neighbour's front door before hearing the sound of a key turning in a lock. Then the door swings open, and I'm suddenly face to face with Steve, the man who once tutted at my husband because he was carrying the shopping bags in from our car instead of making me do it.

'Hello?' Steve says with intonation in his voice as if he's unsure why we are here.

'Hi mate. How's it going?' Sam replies chirpily with a very generous use of the word "mate". These two men are definitely not mates, and their relationship doesn't extend to more than a few grunts about football results over the garden fence whenever they're both in their back gardens. But my husband needs something from Steve today, so I guess "mate" is the right word for this occasion.

'I'm fine,' Steve replies, and I notice him looking me up and down as if I'm on a TV screen and not standing right here looking back at him.

'Great. Sorry to bother you, but we were just wondering if you could help us. We had a visitor last night. Or it could have been a few people. Kids, most likely. But they made a bit of a nuisance, only I didn't get a good look at them, and I was wondering if your camera might have picked them up.'

Sam nods in the direction of the small black camera that is fixed to the wall above the door to Steve's garage. It looks out across his driveway where he has a couple of BMWs parked, but from what Sam has said, it also covers the pavement and some of the road too. Apparently, Steve was bragging about it over the garden fence a while back and saying how good it was for home security.

'You want to look at my camera?' Steve asks, taking a few seconds to catch up with what was a rather basic suggestion.

'That's right,' Sam says. 'If that would be okay? We might be able to stop these kids if they come around again. Who knows, they might come to your place next time.'

I notice how easily Sam is fibbing to our neighbour, and while it is serving its purpose here, it does concern me a little because I never thought of him as being a good liar, yet here he is spouting out a false story as if it's the most casual thing in the world.

If he can do this then what else could he have lied about?

'I can have a look and let you know if I see anything,' Steve suggests, which is rather helpful but might take some time, which doesn't really suit us because we need answers faster than that.

'Is there any chance we could just come in and have a look with you? It's just we know what time it all happened, and it'll probably be a lot quicker if we help. We don't want to waste too much of your time.'

Sam is being very persuasive.

'Err, I dunno. The missus has just got out of the shower. I'll have to check if she's decent.'

'That's okay. We can wait a minute,' Sam tells him, and Steve shrugs before disappearing inside his house and leaving us waiting by his open front door.

I look at my husband, and he gives me a smile as if to say that everything will be fine and we'll be inside checking the camera footage in a moment. I notice that he does seem relaxed, and that makes me feel a little better because I feel like if he had anything to hide about this woman then he wouldn't be behaving like this. He'd most likely be trying to get me to forget all about her.

Thirty seconds later and Steve comes back, looking a little annoyed about things but surprisingly polite enough to not tell us to get lost.

'Come in,' he mumbles in our general direction, and we do as he says, stepping into his home and closing the door.

This is the first time that I have ever been in my next-door neighbours' house, although I'm hardly going to pop round for a cup of tea when the guy who lives here hates women and thinks they exist purely to serve the needs of men. As if on cue to remind me of his personality, Steve tells us both that his wife will be down in a moment if we would like a cup of tea before he leads us through his living room towards the back room where I assume the CCTV footage is stored.

As I walk through the home, I realise that it is exactly the same layout as mine, except everything is in the opposite place. Instead of being on the left, it's on the right. The staircase. The fireplace. The archway into the dining room. It's like a mirror image of my own home, although not as tastefully decorated, I might add. Of course, I'm not going to say that to Steve or his wife, who incidentally has now joined us and obeyed her husband's command to "get the kettle on, love."

As the kettle boils, Steve logs on to the laptop in the room which I guess passes for his study, although there are more car magazines than leather-bound books, and I'm pretty sure I can see a large pair of breasts on a calendar hanging on the wall in the far corner. We use this same room in our home as a den, and there is a TV and sofa in there, but we don't use it as much as we should.

'So what time was it?' Steve asks when he has brought up the software that allows him to look at the footage that his outdoor camera recorded.

'Just after eight,' Sam replies, and Steve does the necessary manoeuvres on his mousepad to get the time on the screen to where we need it to be.

When he does, he clicks the play button, and the screen is suddenly filled with a surprisingly clear recording of Steve's driveway and the road beyond. I can see his two cars sitting on the drive as well as the streetlamp at the end of it. Because I know that the mystery woman walked past Steve's house after she dropped her bombshell in my lap, I'd say there is a good chance that his camera will have captured her.

A few minutes go by as the three of us stare at the screen and watch the seconds ticking away on the counter at the bottom, and Steve's wife interrupts us with her arrival to give us all a cup of tea. I thank her and am just about to take a sip when I see her.

'There she is!' I say, pointing at the screen, although it's not really necessary. She's the only person in the footage, so we could hardly miss her.

'I thought you said it was kids,' Steve says, but Sam and I ignore him and move in closer to the screen to get a better look.

'Can you zoom in?' Sam asks hopefully, but Steve shakes his head as he takes a swig of his tea.

'Nope. That's as good as it gets.'

But that's okay because the footage is sharp and as Steve hits the pause button, Sam and I are able to see the woman clearly.

‘Do you recognise her?’ I ask my husband, and he takes a few seconds to answer me before shaking his head.

‘No. I don’t.’

That’s disappointing because, without a name to put to the face, I have no idea how we could find out any more about this woman.

‘Is that all you need?’ Steve asks us, clearly having had enough of the pair of us already and presumably wanting his home back to himself. I imagine he has got something else for his wife to run around and do for him now.

‘Yeah,’ Sam says before letting out a sigh. ‘I guess that’s it.’

9

SAM

We've just got back from our neighbour's house, but while I went there in hope, I have returned home in disappointment.

That's because I didn't recognise the woman in the CCTV footage.

It was a stroke of genius on my behalf to think of Steve's camera and check out the recording, but it amounted to little because while we did spot the woman leaving, I have no idea who she is. So I guess that's it then. I might never know her name, and more importantly, I might never know why she decided to come to my house and tell my wife that she slept with me.

Rebecca hasn't said too much since we got back from Steve's, and I guess she is feeling as flat as I am about all of this. There's not much else we can do now but try and move on. That would be easy enough to do if it wasn't for the fact that the mystery woman has given my wife a reason to doubt me where no reason used to exist. As much as Rebecca tells me that she is okay and that she believes me when I say I didn't stray, I can't read her mind and see what she is thinking. I hate the idea that she is now consumed with paranoid thoughts about our time together, wondering if I have been as honest as she used to think I was. I also hate the fact that there may be doubt in her mind whenever I stay out late with friends one night or work away from home on business on those rare occasions that I need to.

Rebecca would never have worried about me hurting her before. But I bet she is now, and that makes me furious because it's not fair on her, and it's definitely not fair on me.

I've done nothing wrong. Neither has Rebecca.

The only person in the wrong here is that woman.

But she has got away scot-free.

So far, this Sunday has been a little different to our usual ones. Instead of newspapers and coffee over the kitchen table, we've been round at Steve's house, which looked a lot like ours although not as tastefully decorated. I'm sure Rebecca noticed that too, but I can't chat to her about it because she has been upstairs ever since we got back, locked away in the bathroom, and I'm not entirely sure what she is doing in there. I did knock a few minutes ago to check that she was okay, and she told me that she was fine, so I left her to it, but I'll feel better when she has come out and I can see for myself.

When she does, I'm going to suggest that we go for a walk and stretch our legs. It will do us good to get out of the house, considering we've been cooped up in it for most of the weekend. It will also do us good to have a break from this place after what happened here last night.

I know it's going to drive me mad not knowing who that woman was and why she did what she did, but

I'm going to have to learn to deal with it somehow because there's little chance of her ever coming back and enlightening us further about her thought process. What might have been a silly game for her could have potentially ruined my marriage and seen me kicked out of the house, so I hope she is having a good laugh, wherever she is. She better hope that I never bump into her because now I know what she looks like, I could very easily spot her and make a scene.

But there is something still bugging me as I sit down on the sofa and wait for Rebecca to come downstairs so we can get on with our Sunday. It's the fact that the woman knew our names. That must mean that she knows us both somehow. But from where? I could drive myself mad trying to think of all the ways that someone might get mine and my wife's name, so I don't want to go down that rabbit hole because it's likely that I'll never figure it out. But it's still bugging me.

I need a drink.

I take out my phone and look up the number for the pub around the corner from here. I know they do a cracking Sunday Roast, and I wonder if I could book a table for us this afternoon. It's short notice, but they might be able to squeeze us in. A good chunk of beef and gravy should cheer us both up and go a little way to helping us put this weekend behind us. I hope in time that this becomes one of those things we both laugh about and maybe even bring up at a dinner party or two.

"Remember that night when a strange woman came to the house, dear?"

"How can I forget? What a weird thing that was!'

I'm sure our friends will be interested to hear about it. They all think we're the perfect couple and that nothing exciting ever happens to us, so I imagine they will get a kick out of the story of the woman at the door. The problem is that while Rebecca and I might laugh at the story one day, there will always be that lingering doubt in our minds about what it was really about.

It's a question that might never be answered.

At least that's not the case for plenty of other questions I could ask.

'Hey, I was wondering if you had a table free this afternoon for food? We can do any time if you can fit us in.'

I listen to the young girl at the other end of the line as she tells me that she will check, and I can just about hear her voice over the din in the background. The pub sounds busy, and I'm not holding out much hope that she will be giving me good news in a few seconds' time. But after the misfortune of last night, it seems like my luck is changing because she tells me that she can fit us in at three o'clock, so I quickly give her my name and number and tell her that we will see her later.

Hanging up the phone, I feel good about what I have just done and not only because I'm starving. It's because Rebecca will appreciate the gesture.

I just need her to hurry up and come down so I can tell her about it.

I hear the toilet flush upstairs and a few floorboards creaking, so I know she is on the move again, which is a relief because I was starting to worry that she was in the bathroom crying her eyes out or something. But then I see her come down the stairs, and while she has obviously done her best to hide it, her eyes are tear-stained.

She has been crying.

'What's wrong?' I ask, getting up from the sofa and rushing to meet my wife at the bottom of the stairs.

'It's okay. I'm just being silly,' she replies, but I'm not buying it.

'What is it? Is it about last night?'

Rebecca shakes her head as if to say no, but she can't control the emotions that overwhelm her, and she starts crying again. As I pull her in for a hug and try to soothe her, I feel the anger rising up inside me at that damn woman and what she has reduced my darling Rebecca to. She's never been a crier, yet here she is now blubbing away on the bottom step of the staircase. So much for a fun weekend before we go back to work.

Thanks to that bitch at the door last night, this has turned into the weekend from hell.

As I stand there with my arms wrapped around my sobbing wife, I make a vow to myself then and there that I am going to find the woman at the door and make her explain herself to me. Better yet, I will make her apologise to Rebecca for causing her so much distress. She can't be allowed to get away with that behaviour. What if my wife had been more fragile? She could have harmed herself after hearing something like that. Nobody expects to open the front door and be told that their partner has cheated on them, yet that's what happened here. If it was true, I would have no one to blame but myself, but it isn't so I'm seething, and I'm only getting more wound up by the minute.

I'm going to find that woman. I don't know how, but I will find her.

Then she will wish that she never came knocking at my door.

10

THE WOMAN

I can see Rebecca and Sam's front door again, but I'm not planning on knocking on it this time. Why bother? I know they're not in.

Besides, I'm more interested in the back door.

Walking fast because it's best not to be seen loitering around outside somebody's house, I go down the couple's driveway and around the side of the property, in the direction of the back garden. I see the gate ahead of me that I knew would be here and I reach over and fiddle for the latch on the other side, just like I did when I completed my trial run earlier in the week.

The gate opens easily, and now I'm in the garden.

It's hardly the most secure gate, but like most things in people's homes, it's just for show. It looks secure, but it's actually not. Its existence can deter most people but not those who know how easy it is to open. I'm constantly amused by how little attention people pay to their home security. Accessing inner-city homes can be a nightmare, but out here in suburbia, it's a doddle. It's as if people see the news and watch all the reports of the terrible things happening in London or Birmingham or Manchester and shake their heads but feel safe because they're not there. They're in some commuter-belt town like Reading or Coventry or Bury, where they feel like nothing bad ever happens.

They think they are safe.

They are wrong.

Rebecca and Sam's back garden is small but pleasant and offers just the right amount of space for what they need. There is a table and chair set on the patio, which I imagine they use to sit out and eat whenever the weather is nice. There is a tiny patch of grass in the middle, which I imagine Sam cuts every few weeks in the summer or whenever Rebecca tells him that it needs doing. And there is a small shed at the bottom of the garden, which I imagine is filled with all sorts of items that never get used but never seem to get thrown away either. But most importantly, there is no camera back here, which means I'm not going to be seen illegally entering this house in a moment's time.

It's irritating how many people have installed cameras outside their homes over recent years, but I was glad to see that Rebecca and Sam were not amongst them when I inspected the exterior of their home before I knocked on their front door. That tells me that they aren't as paranoid as some other members of society, or at least not about crime anyway. But I imagine they are paranoid about other things right now, mainly who I am and if I'll ever come calling at their house again.

But like I said, while I am calling again today, I know that neither of them are in. It's a Monday morning, and both homeowners are at work. Rebecca will be in the site offices at the construction company where she is employed as an engineer while Sam will be in his office in the centre of London where he works as a consultant. Neither of them will be back home until tonight, but I don't need anywhere near as much time as that to get in and get out of their house.

I will only be here for a short time.

But I will plant something here that will cause problems for a long time.

Reaching the back door, I take out the key that I use for door locks just like this one and slide it into the lock. This process is called 'bumping' and all it requires to make happen is purchasing a special modified key online and using a screwdriver to gently bump it when it is in the lock. An amateur might leave evidence behind in the form of damage to the lock, but I'm not an amateur. I've done this enough times to get it right because it's not just about getting in.

It's about making sure that nobody knows I was in.

The door easily unlocks when I turn the key, as it should do, and now I'm in. It's as easy as that, but it's not all easy.

I still have to disable the house alarm.

Walking quickly towards the beeping white box on the wall in the hallway, I know that I have twenty seconds until the full alarm is activated. That's the one that all the neighbours will be able to hear if it goes off, so it's important to me that it doesn't. But this is a common home security system that I have seen plenty of times before, so I know where the weaknesses are. That's how I'm able to enter the code that makes it turn off instantly. It's not the code that Rebecca and Sam use to program it, but it is the code the manufacturers of this alarm used when it was configured, and it still works.

Nobody is supposed to know about it.

But I know.

With the alarm dealt with, the beeping sound ceases, and the house is silent. Just the way I like it. Now I'm free to carry out the rest of my work in peace, and I do just that, heading upstairs and into the master bedroom where I take out the item of clothing in my coat pocket. Then I start opening drawers in the bedroom, looking for a particular one. It doesn't take me long to find it. I find most women keep their underwear in a top drawer close to the bed, and Rebecca is no different.

I put the new item of underwear inside, hidden amongst the items that were already there and then close the drawer so that nobody knows it has been tampered with. Then I go to the wardrobe and open it, looking for Sam's shirts which I expect to be hanging in here somewhere. Sure enough, there they are, several of them, all different colours and all very smart. These are the shirts he wears to work, and I can see that he would look very dashing in all of these. I decide to take out the white one and open up the collar on it before taking out an item of makeup from my pocket and getting artistic for a moment. Then I put the collar back down on the shirt and return it to its rightful place in the wardrobe, so it looks like it was never removed.

With my work here complete, I make one final check on the bedroom to ensure that my presence here has not been obvious before leaving the room and heading back downstairs. Using the manufacturers' reset code to secure the house again, I escape out of the back door in the twenty seconds I have before the alarm activates and use my key to lock up behind me. Then all I have to do is go back through the side gate, close that and head away down the street to get on with the rest of my day.

I love what I do for work, and I love what other people do for work too.

While they're out all day doing their job, I get to sneak into their homes and do mine.

Who said Monday mornings were dull?

11

REBECCA

I hate Mondays. Time seems to be standing still, and that is not something anybody wants to happen when they are at work. As usual, the weekend went far too quickly, and now I'm back here again in a freezing cold cabin in the middle of a field on a building site.

Some days, I love my job as an engineer and other days, I hate it.

Today, I hate it.

I enjoy the mental stimulation that comes with this role, as well as the unpredictability of it and the fact that I'm not always chained to a desk for eight hours a day. At any point, I can get up from here, put on my hard hat and my hi-viz jacket and go out on site to make a few checks and chat to a few of the workers. That's a luxury when the weather is nice.

It's not so great when it's raining.

I even enjoy working in such a male-dominated industry as construction. Sure, the conversations in the canteen are a little different to what they would be if I worked with mostly women, but I have always got on well with men. I like how straightforward they are. There's no bitchiness, gossiping or secrets. Men, or at least the ones I work with, just say it as it is. That is very refreshing, and I like working in an environment like this one.

I also like the fact that I don't have to put on a load of makeup or fret over what to wear to the office each day in case I get judged by any female colleagues. Here, muddy boots and scruffy hair are as common a sight in the office as a computer and a coffee machine, and that's fine by me. I save my beautifying for the weekends. During the week, I'm just Rebecca, a site engineer with mud on her clothes and knots in her hair. At the weekends, I'm a more feminine version of myself because as much as my husband loves me, I'm not sure he gets turned on by dirty boots and bright green jackets with concrete splattered across them.

I've been an engineer for fifteen years, after graduating from university and taking on my first role on a site. The years have flown by since then, although in some ways, they haven't because there has been plenty of slow mornings just like this one to get through along the way. Checking the time at the bottom of my computer screen, I see that it is only 10:02. God, this day is dragging already. I just want to go home and get into bed. It's not unusual for me to feel tired after the weekend, but this was not a normal weekend by any stretch of the imagination.

The woman at the door on Saturday night saw to that.

I haven't slept properly since then, my mind ablaze with all sorts of thoughts and worries about my husband, that woman and what it might mean to my previously happy life. Not even a Sunday Roast in a pub yesterday afternoon could take my mind off things. It was sweet of Sam to take me out for a meal, and the food was fantastic, as it always is when we go to that particular venue. It's just that it's difficult to truly appreciate beef, potatoes and gravy when all you can think about is some other woman with your man.

I can't get the image of that woman out of my mind, and that fact hasn't been helped by going to our neighbours' house yesterday and looking at her on his CCTV footage. Having to see that blonde hair, those red lips and that pair of high heels for a second time has only reinforced the image of her that I have in my mind and in turn, it's only making me feel worse.

It's not untrue to say that the woman is more attractive than me. And it's not untrue to say that I could see how my husband would like her if indeed what she told me was true about them sleeping together. Maybe I took my eye off the ball. Maybe coming home every night from site dirty and dishevelled has slowly turned Sam onto another woman.

What man prefers his woman to opt for mud over makeup?

Damn these paranoid thoughts. Will they ever leave me alone now? If only I hadn't answered that door. If only I had stayed on the sofa with Sam eating Indian food and watching that film. Things were so perfect then, or at least I thought they were. But now, things feel like they are falling apart.

I broke down in front of my husband yesterday. I'd locked myself in the bathroom for as long as I could and hoped that I'd gotten all the tears out in private but no sooner had I gone downstairs and seen him again then the floodgates reopened, and I ended up blubbing into his shoulder. I thought I was strong enough to keep it together and not let what that woman said affect me. I thought I was okay in trusting my husband and believing his word over hers. But I guess not, and now I fear that things are never going to be the same again.

Peace of mind is taken for granted until you no longer have it. I think back to all the days I used to sit here in this site office looking out of the window at the excavators and the men in their hard hats, and while I was a little bored, I was never worried. But now I'm worried. I'm worried all the time. I'm worried because of what that woman told me.

I'm worried that I can't trust the man I call my husband.

Whenever I feel like time isn't moving, I grab my jacket and my hat and get up out of my seat, leaving the stuffy office behind for a walk in the fresh air around the site. So that is what I will do now, even if it is raining out there and I don't technically need to go outside for anything. I'm hoping that by distracting my mind then time will speed up, and more importantly, I'll stop thinking about Sam being with that woman.

Leaving the site cabin, I trudge across the muddy car park in the direction of the building site across the dirt track. Passing all the expensive company cars that the managers have driven here today before going inside to the warm site office, I make my way over to where the real workers around here are toiling away in the wind and rain. I nod at a couple of guys as they pass me, our expressions indicating how wild this weather is and how unlucky we are to be out in it. But I don't actually feel unlucky. I'm glad of the distraction. It's hard to worry about anything, even potential infidelity in a marriage, when there are huge machines moving around nearby and large holes that could easily be fallen into. It's imperative to stay focused when in a dangerous environment like this one, and that is what I will do.

I will not think about that woman at the door while I am out here.

I will not think about Sam or how upset I got yesterday.

I will just think about doing my job. That's all I can control.

My home life is personal. This is work, and I should keep the two separate.

Walking around an excavated pit with several exposed pipes running through it, I make my way towards the cabin on the other side of this building site. That is where I will find Frank, the friendly old chap who sits in there and hands out personal protective equipment to the site workers, as well as keeping a log of all the tools that go in and out. While it might not look like it, almost everything on this site is extremely expensive, so it's the job of Frank to make sure that it's all monitored and doesn't go missing. Last year, we had to fire a couple of guys after we found out they had been stealing tools and selling them off privately.

It's crazy what people will do for money.

It's also crazy what people will do for love.

Despite my best intentions, I am thinking about Sam and that woman again. Am I being blind to the truth that is staring me right in the face? Did he cheat on me? Was that woman just a genuine person who felt I deserved to know the truth?

Am I making a mistake in trying to carry on as if everything is okay?

I'm not sure, but one thing is clear. I am making a mistake by daydreaming while walking through the middle of a busy construction site. That's how I ended up missing the call from the foreman when he tried to warn me that I was stepping into the blind spot of a small excavator nearby. The machine was moving but so was I, and it was only at the last second when I saw it reversing towards me.

If it hadn't been for the quick thinking of a site worker who pulled me out of the way at the last second then I could have been crushed by that machine. Thankfully, I just ended up on the floor covered in mud and feeling a little shaken up.

But I could have been killed.

That was a warning.

It's a warning that I can't carry on like this.

I have to know the truth about that woman.

12

SAM

The first day of the working week is over, and I am grateful for that. Just four more days to go until Rebecca and I are sitting on our sofa again on Saturday night eating delicious food and watching the latest film release. I guess they call it "living for the weekend", but I'm not that bad. I do enjoy my job, and it's good to have a structure and routine that involves more than eating and watching TV. But there's no denying that the weekends are better than the weekdays.

So roll on Saturday.

That's not the only thing I need to roll on. The traffic sitting in front of me on this busy road needs to get rolling too, but so far, very little is moving. A traffic jam is the last thing that I need after a busy day in the office. It's also the last thing I need for my empty stomach, which is rumbling away and will continue to do so until I get home and put some food into it. I wonder if Rebecca has finished work before me tonight. Maybe she is home and already has something cooking in the oven. That would be lovely, but I'm not banking on it. Unlike Steve, my sexist neighbour, I don't believe that a woman's place is in the kitchen. It's wherever that woman wants to be, and I know Rebecca wants to be on a building site full of men, which is a little amusing but each to their own.

I'm proud of my wife and what she does for a living. I also think it's a little badass that she goes to work in boots and a helmet. Some of my friends tease me and ask if I would prefer it if she wore dresses and short skirts like some of their partners when they go to work, but I just laugh and tell them that I don't care. I love my wife no matter how she looks. All I care about is that she is happy, and I know she is much happier on a building site getting covered in mud than she would be sitting behind a desk looking prim and proper and trying not to break a nail on her keyboard.

It's the thought of Rebecca's happiness that makes me feel that knot of anxiety in my stomach again as I sit here in this heavy traffic and wait for something to move. Seeing my wife crying in front of me yesterday was devastating, and I know that she was still distracted when we went to the pub and had our meal. I wonder how she has got on today at work. I really hope she hasn't been thinking about that bloody woman who came to our door and told a vicious lie. I also hope she hasn't got too wet out on site today.

I always think of my wife when it rains because I know that she hates it in her line of work. But it has been drizzling all day, and the raindrops are coming down harder now, bouncing off my windscreen and forcing me to increase the speed of the wipers as they try to fend the water off so I can see where I am going. Not that it matters where I am going because this road is still gridlocked, and I'm no nearer to getting back to my warm house where a fully-stocked fridge is just waiting to be raided.

I'm just about to turn on the radio and see if I can find some good music to help pass the time when I hear the ringing alert that is built into my car that lets me know that somebody is calling me. I press the button on my steering wheel that activates the hands-free system, and it automatically answers the call for me, allowing me to talk without picking up my device and keeping me on the right side of British law, which decrees that drivers of cars are not allowed to touch their phones when at the wheel.

'Hello?' I say as I watch the raindrops bouncing off my windscreen.

'Hey, Sam. It's Maria. You okay to talk?'

'Yeah, go for it.'

I've not exactly got anything else to do while I'm sitting here in traffic, have I? So why not take a call from my colleague who I have just spent the last three hours sitting in a meeting with as we tried to figure out the payment terms on a new deal that our business is brokering with a client.

'I was just looking at the figures again, and I'm not sure we're going to be able to make clause seventeen work. I can put it all on an email, but I just thought I'd give you a heads up before you see it and start to cry.'

I laugh at Maria's joke. I definitely won't be crying, but she's not far off. From what she is saying, she has just found another problem in the initial problem that we have spent all afternoon trying to solve.

'Great. Send it over to me, and I'll grab a box of tissues before I start reading,' I reply, and I hear the sound of Maria's laughter at the other end of the line.

She is from Spain, and while she speaks good English, her accent can mean it can be difficult to understand her sometimes. It's usually worst whenever she is presenting, probably because she gets nervous and talks really fast, meaning it's even harder to decipher what she is saying. At least that's the polite explanation for not hearing her sometimes. The more impolite version that many guys in the office claim to be true is that she is so attractive that it's not her words they are paying attention to.

As a married man, I'm not going to speak too much on the beauty of any woman who isn't my wife, but there are plenty of guys in my office who are happy to do so, and the general consensus is that she is smoking hot. But that doesn't matter, at least not in the workplace anyway. What matters is that she is a damn good consultant and does a great job for our company. She must be because how else could she have risen to such a good position by her mid-thirties? She knows her stuff, and she actually knows more than me, although I try not to make that too obvious in our meetings.

'I've just sent it,' Maria says in her Spanish lilt. 'Let me know what you think. Have a good evening.'

'Thanks. You too.'

I push the button on my steering wheel to end the call, and now the only sound in my vehicle is the rain hitting the windscreen again. I guess I've got an email to read over when I get home. Great. And there I was looking forward to a quiet evening in front of the TV with Rebecca. At least the traffic has started to move again. I should be home soon, and then I can do something about my growling stomach. I can also do something to set my nerves at ease a little. I can see if Rebecca is really okay after the events of the weekend. I really hope she is. I've got enough on my plate with work, and by the sounds of Maria's call, even more has been added to it. I could do without my personal life being a problem too. That's why I hope that Rebecca is okay and that she's had a good day. Or just a boring day. As long as it's been normal.

No drama. No incident. No bloody woman at the front door.

Just a plain old boring Monday.

Fingers crossed.

13

REBECCA

I've been home since lunchtime, not long after I was dragged away from behind the heavy wheels of a ten-tonne machine that could easily have ended my life. I was shaken up after the incident, just like anyone else would be, so I was allowed to go home after I'd been seen by the Health and Safety Officer on site.

I'm physically fine, and no harm was done in the end, but that doesn't mean it doesn't need to be investigated by my colleagues. I feel bad for creating paperwork for them and also for the fact that what happened has to be logged as a "near-miss," which is not something that is generally well-received in health and safety circles. Managers will have to meet and discuss what happened and why in order to ensure that something like that can't happen again. Blame will also have to be attributed somewhere, but there is no one to blame for what happened but me.

It's my fault I was walking across a busy building site in a daydream, and it's my fault that I almost got killed by a reversing excavator.

I owned up to my mistake as soon as it happened and made sure that nobody else could face punishment for the incident. But still, it's not a good look for me, my career and the career of anybody who is in charge of maintaining safety on the site.

There was a large number scribbled on the whiteboard in the site canteen which everybody who worked there got to see on a daily basis. It was the number to show how many accidents or near-misses had occurred since construction began. Ever since the project started six months ago, that number has been zero. But now it has changed.

Now it is a number one, and I am responsible for that.

I'm a bloody statistic.

Site managers will lose recommendations and bonuses because that number didn't stay at zero for the entirety of the project.

All because of me and my silly behaviour.

All because I was too distracted thinking about that woman at the door.

Now I'm at home lying on the bed even though it's barely six, and I never go horizontal this early. On a normal day, I'd either be in the kitchen preparing something for dinner or I'd be at the gym working up a sweat after a busy day on site. I'd be active. I'd be useful. I'd be normal. Yet here I am, being of no use to anybody. All because some stranger told me something that may or may not be true on Saturday night.

I hear the sound of keys in the front door downstairs. Sam's home. That means it's only a few seconds until he sees that I'm home too. He won't be shocked about that, but he will be shocked to see me lying on the bed. He'll want to know why. He'll want to know if I'm okay.

So what am I going to tell him?

I hear the front door close, and his car keys drop onto the small table in the hallway, and then I hear him call out to me. I'm tempted to jump off the bed quickly and pretend that everything is okay. Maybe I don't have to tell him about the near-miss at work. Maybe he never has to know that his wife was very nearly squashed today. But it's not fair to lie. Not for him or for me. Honesty is the most important element in any successful marriage, so I have to be honest. There is no other choice.

Just like Sam is being honest with me?

I have to hope so.

'Hi, love. I'm up here!' I call out to him, and I hear his footsteps climbing the staircase a few seconds later.

I bet he's starving, and I wonder if he's disappointed that I haven't started cooking anything. Possibly but he would never say anything if so. He doesn't expect me to have dinner on the table for him every night when he gets home.

Unlike Steve.

His poor wife must live in their kitchen.

Having decided to be upfront and honest with Sam, I stay on the bed until he has entered the room, not making any attempt to pretend like I haven't had a bad day at work.

'Are you okay?' he asks as soon as he spots me.

'Yeah, I'm fine. But there was almost an accident on site.'

'What?' Sam cries, rushing towards me and sitting on the bed beside me. 'What happened?'

'It was stupid. I wasn't paying attention to where I was going and almost walked into the path of an excavator.'

'You did what?'

'I'm fine. But it had to go down as a near miss, and they sent me home for the day.'

'Are you in trouble?'

'No, nothing like that. It's just to make sure I'm okay and not in shock or anything like that.'

'Jesus, was it that bad?'

'I had to be dragged out of the way.'

'Oh my God, Rebecca. Are you serious?'

I shrug and nod my head.

'How did this happen? Why weren't you paying attention to where you were going?'

'I don't know. I guess with what happened this weekend, I've been finding it hard to concentrate on other things.'

Sam goes quiet at that, and I wonder what he is thinking.

'But there's no harm done, and it won't happen again,' I add, hoping that will stop him worrying about me.

'This is ridiculous. I'm going to call the police.'

I watch as Sam takes out his mobile phone.

'What are you talking about? What have the police got to do with anything?'

'You almost died today because you were reeling from what that lying woman said to you. I can't have this. We have to find out who she was and why she did it.'

'Sam, it's fine, really. I'm okay.'

I'm surprised at how wound up my husband has got, and he really does look like he wants to call the police. But that is silly and not at all what I want. What would he say to them when they arrived? *"Hi, officers. Sorry to bother you, but my wife almost died today because she was being stupid and not paying attention. But it's not her fault. It's the fault of a stranger who knocked on our door a couple of nights ago and said I was cheating on her."*

I can't imagine the police officers will be too thrilled about having their time wasted on a silly thing like that. That's why I take the phone from my husband's hand and toss it across the bed so he can't call 999 with it.

'What are you doing?' he asks me, clearly still riled up after the shock of what I have just told him happened to me today.

'I don't want you to call the police. And I don't want to think about that woman anymore. I just want things to go back to normal. I trust you, and I promise I won't let any of my paranoid thoughts put me in danger again.'

Sam listens to everything I am telling him, but I'm not sure he is really taking it on board. That's because he looks back at his phone again as if anxious to still make that call.

‘I mean it,’ I say, taking his hand and pulling it towards me. ‘I’m okay. Saturday night was a shock, and it’s taken me a few days to get my head around it, but I’m going to be fine. We’re going to be fine. That’s because she was lying, wasn’t she? The woman at the door. She was lying, right?’

‘Of course she was lying.’

I nod my head because that’s the last thing I needed to hear on the matter.

‘Good. Now, how about some dinner? Shall we be naughty and have a takeaway on a Monday?’

Sam gives me a wry smile, and it’s clear that he is keen too. That’s why I allow him to pick up his mobile phone again and make a call, only this time it is to the local Chinese restaurant and not the local police station. I’m happy for him to answer the door to a man clutching a bag of prawn crackers in an hour’s time. I’m just glad he won’t be answering it to a couple of police officers.

And let’s hope we never have to answer it to that woman again either.

14

SAM

It's a pleasant surprise to be eating a Chinese takeaway on a Monday night. There are certainly worse ways to start the week. But it was not a pleasant surprise to come home and find out that Rebecca was almost involved in a fatal accident at work today. It was even more galling to learn that it happened because of what went down with that woman on Saturday night.

If I was determined to find out who she was before, I am even more dedicated now.

I still have some of my food left, but I stop eating, not because I'm full but because I'm too distracted to concentrate and enjoy it.

'Have you had enough?' Rebecca asks me when she notices that I have put down my knife and fork.

'Yeah. I might save the rest for lunch tomorrow,' I say. 'Gives me something to look forward to during the morning.'

Rebecca laughs and decides that she will do the same with hers, and two minutes later, the leftover food is back in its containers and chilling in the fridge where it will stay overnight.

'Do you want to watch something?' Rebecca asks me, but I tell her about that work email I need to read, and she doesn't mind, saying that she fancied an early night anyway and heading for the stairs.

I tell her that I will be up shortly before giving her a kiss and heading into the kitchen, where I sit down at the table with my laptop and open it up. But even though I do need to read that email from Maria, it's not work that I'm concerning myself with now.

Instead, I'm going to look for ways to track someone down.

I know it's not going to be easy. For a start, I'm going to have to ask Steve if I can have a recording of that CCTV footage that he got on Saturday night so that I can give it to whoever I hire to try and find out who that woman is. But I have to do something. I had already decided to try and find out, but after what happened to Rebecca today, I'm not going to give up until I do.

But it's not just about my wife's paranoia surrounding this woman and what it might mean for our marriage. It's about my paranoia too. I'm worried that this person might come back again, and she could say anything to Rebecca. She is clearly capable of lying, so who knows what else she is capable of telling her? What if this woman comes back and tells Rebecca that she is seeing me again or that I am planning on leaving her? Of course, it will all be lies, but Rebecca doesn't know that for sure. She'll worry, and she'll be distracted. That could lead to another incident like today, only this time, she might not be so lucky.

As for me, how can I feel settled in my relationship knowing that there is a threat out there in the world who could come back at any minute and drop another bombshell? That woman had no right to make up a lie about me and risk everything that I have worked hard to build for myself. This home. This marriage. This life. She could have ruined everything, and for what? What could she have possibly hoped to achieve by spreading a lie into my home? I bet she never thought that someone might die, but that's what has almost happened, and now it's gone too far.

That's why I have to do this.

I have to find this woman.

And I have to do it now.

Without any expertise in this area, I am taking to opening up a search engine on my computer screen and typing in the words 'private investigator'. I don't know if a PI is really what I need, but I'll do some reading and find out. What I do need is somebody who has the means of doing a little digging and uncovering the truth. It might not be cheap, and it might not end up being entirely legal, but right now, I don't care about cheap and legal. I just care about my wife, and I care about finding the woman who put my wife into such a spin that she almost ended up being run over by a machine.

The search results bring up a few websites, and I do a little exploring, clicking on a few of the links and seeing where they take me. I see numerous sites set up for PI's, all of whom are offering their services on all manner of things.

Monitor a cheating spouse. Track down a long-lost relative. Verify information.

There's no mention of identifying a stranger, but all these types of services essentially aim to do the same thing, which is uncover the truth, and that is all I'm looking to do.

I just want the truth.

The truth is a concept that the woman at the door clearly has no regard for. But the truth means a lot to me, and I know it means a lot to my wife too. That is why I am going to do everything I can to reveal it.

After ten minutes of browsing various sites belonging to various private investigators, I realise that I'm just going to have to pick one and go with it. There is very little to help me make that choice because this isn't like shopping for a product. There aren't any reviews, and there aren't any prices. It's all very secretive and murky.

In the end, I pick one website and scroll down to the bottom where I click on the button that says *"Contact me for a quote today."*

It opens up a small box in which I have to input my email address and mobile number as well as a short message about what it is that I am hoping to achieve with the help of a PI. I add my contact information in the boxes before typing out the job that I require. I'm not really sure what to put, so I just write from the heart.

Hi. My wife and I were visited by a female stranger a couple of nights ago, and she told a very damaging lie. I would like to find out who this woman was and why she did that. I have camera footage of the woman that I can send, but that's all I have to go on. Can you help find this person? Regards. Sam.

I re-read the message quickly to check for typos before clicking the send button. The confirmation message on screen tells me that my submission was successful and that I will be contacted shortly. I guess all I can do now is wait.

I'm just about to close down the laptop when I remember about that work email that I was supposed to look at tonight. It's still relatively early in the evening, so I log onto my company intranet and access my emails. Finding the one from Maria, I open it up and start reading, feeling the life drain out of me as I do. Maria was right. There is a problem with one of the terms, and it's going to take another long meeting to sort it out.

Tomorrow is going to be fun. *Not.*

I hit 'Reply' on the email and type out a quick message to my colleague telling her that she is right and that she has done well to spot the problem. Then I conclude with a sarcastic joke, saying that I can't wait for tomorrow and that it promises to be one of the most exciting days in our careers. But just before I send it, I have a moment of doubt. What if Maria doesn't get the sarcasm and thinks I'm being serious. Or worse, what if she doesn't find it funny and thinks I'm weird? I know she speaks English, but she might not get the English humour over email, so that's why I decide to delete it and just keep it simple. Then I press send, and the message whizzes away into the ether.

But as I close my laptop down, I'm struck by a thought. Why did I care so much if Maria got my joke or not? It hardly matters. Yet I did care. I cared enough to change my entire message. I'm not sure why I did that.

It's not as if I'm trying to impress her. Not like all the other guys in the office. But maybe I am. I must be if I was worried about what she would think of me.

Never mind. It's not important. What is important is finding that mystery woman. But that won't happen until the private investigator messages me back, so all I can do until then is go upstairs and be with my wife.

It's been a long day.

And it's only Monday.

Give me strength.

15

THE WOMAN

I'm one of those lucky people who enjoy what they do for a living, so I don't need to concern myself with what day of the week it is and how long is left until the weekend. I can't wait to go to work every day.

The only problem I have is that there just isn't enough work around.

What I do is quite specialist. I'm not sure how many other people around the world have the same business as I do. I certainly don't have any colleagues. I do this very much on my own, and that is vital because what I do is dangerous.

I play with people's lives.

Of course, I don't do that for the fun of it. I command a hefty fee, a figure that my prospective clients are often shocked at when I first give it to them. But I don't charge a lot out of greed.

I charge a lot because I risk a lot.

Take Rebecca and Sam, for example. I've had to sneak into their home, and I could have been caught at any moment. That would have resulted in a prison sentence and a criminal record. That's why I charge a lot. I need to be well compensated in case something goes wrong. But so far, nothing has ever gone wrong. My assignments have always gone well, my clients have always been happy, and most importantly, I have avoided prison. I can't complain. But I'm only human, so I can always find something to complain about, and that is why I'm complaining about not having enough business.

I can sometimes go days without work, and while that doesn't matter financially because I have plenty of money from my previous jobs, it matters when it comes to keeping myself busy. It's like I have the best job in the world, but I just can't do it all the time. It's very frustrating, but I guess that is perhaps the price to pay for being ahead of my time. As I said, I don't know anyone else who does what I do. It's not that there isn't a market for it. It's just that it's very niche, and most importantly, it's very hard to advertise. I can't just put up a billboard or run a commercial. My success in keeping my business away from the prying eyes of the police is down to discretion. All my clients have to sign an agreement that says they will never disclose what I do in the event of it being uncovered. That keeps me safe, but it also keeps them safe too. They are just as guilty as I am.

The only difference between us is I get rich while they get the chance to snare the man or woman of their dreams.

Here's how it works. A prospective client will contact me and tell me their story. It's nearly always the same story, and the only things that change are the names. Here's an example. Say there's a woman called Sarah and she is in love with a man called Simon. Now Sarah could just tell Simon that she likes him and ask him out for a drink, but there is just one problem. Simon is married to Stella, and he's a good guy, so he's not going to cheat or leave his wife. So what can Sarah do? Give up on her heart's desire and find somebody else to fall in love with or get serious about what she really wants?

If she gives up, she has no one to blame but herself.

But if she gets serious, that's when she gives me a call.

It's at that point that Sarah will give me Simon and Stella's names, as well as their address, and that's when I go to work learning everything that I can about them.

Their habits. Their routines.

Their weaknesses.

Then it's just a case of implementing a series of strategies that will yield the result that my client requires. And what does the client require? In Sarah's case, she wants Simon and Stella to break up. That way, she will have a chance at getting her man once he is unencumbered. But why would Simon and Stella break up if they were happily married?

Because I can make it seem like one of them is cheating on the other.

All I have to do is plant some seeds and watch them grow. The first thing to do is create doubt in the subject's mind. Stella might think of her husband as being loyal until she suddenly sees me on her doorstep telling her that he is not. I have no evidence to give, but I don't need it at that time. All I needed to do was plant the first seed. Now Stella is thinking about it, and the first crack in the solid foundation of their marriage has been made.

Then I simply create more cracks by planting things in their house, things that shouldn't be there. I can also use technology to create messages that seem incriminating for a cheating spouse or send handwritten letters with even more fake claims in them. In truth, I can do anything that I want because I'm the boss of my own business, and that business is all about understanding what makes human beings tick.

Hope. Fear. Happiness. Paranoia. We're all the same, and we all want the same thing.

We just want to be loved.

That's the concept that marriages are built on. Two people who love each other and make a commitment to be together forever. But those marriages only work with trust, and losing that trust can bring the whole thing crumbling down.

In the end, Stella will leave Simon because she can't trust him. It doesn't matter that he has done nothing wrong because the evidence I left has created enough distrust for things to never be the same again. Then my work is done, but for my client, Sarah, her job is just beginning. Now it's up to her to make all that time, money and effort worth it by swooping in and taking Simon for himself, preferably when he's feeling at his lowest point after the breakdown of his marriage and needs somebody to cheer him up.

And just like that, Sarah has got her dream man.

She's happy because she's always loved him, Simon's happy because he has a new woman to make him feel good about himself, and I'm happy because I'm thousands of pounds richer. The only person who isn't happy in the end is Stella, but not everyone can be a winner. But she'll move on and find somebody new eventually, so I don't spend too much time worrying about her.

That's my business. That's how it works. And that's exactly what I am doing to Rebecca and Sam right now for my client. I am planting seeds. I am creating distrust. And I am about to bring their whole marriage tumbling down.

How exciting.

Is it any wonder that I can't wait to get back to work?

16

REBECCA

I'm glad it's Friday because that means work is over for another week. But as every female knows, a woman's work is never done, and so it proves now because while I have finished at my workplace, I still have plenty of chores to be getting on with around the home. The first task is to put a wash on, so I pick up the basket in the bedroom and carry it downstairs. Working in construction tends to mean an early finish on a Friday, and I've always enjoyed that about the industry. In my younger days, it would mean that I was able to start drinking earlier than my other friends ahead of our Friday nights out, but now that I'm older and somewhat more sensible, it simply means I can get home quicker and get some menial tasks out of the way so that I don't have to do them on the weekend. Nobody wants to do dirty washing, but it has to be done, so I might as well get it out of the way.

But I'm not completely boring these days. I do have more exciting plans tonight after the chores are done. Sam and I are going out with one of my best friends and her partner for a meal, and it should be fun. But before the fun comes the chores.

Reaching the utility room, I put the basket down and take off the lid before pulling out the dirty garments inside and tossing them into the washing machine. I've decided to do a white wash, so I filter the clothes going into the machine, making sure that I don't make a mistake and put something colourful in there. It's mainly Sam's work shirts that are going in, and I roll down the sleeves and open up the collars on all of them so that they get a thorough wash during the cycle. But it's as I am opening up the collar on the third white shirt that I'm about to put into the machine when I see it.

A red mark on the collar.

Lipstick?

It certainly looks that way. But how has lipstick come to be on my husband's shirt? It certainly isn't mine because I don't wear lipstick during the week and that's when Sam wears these shirts. It must have come from somebody else. But who? And how did it get on here?

I know it's important not to overreact and read too much into something because the chances are that it has a simple and innocent explanation, but these are not simple or fully innocent times. This is still the same week that a woman came to my door and told me that my husband had cheated on me. While that was shocking, there was no evidence anywhere at all to back up that claim.

But now there might be.

I decide to keep the suspicious shirt out of the wash so that I can show it to Sam when he gets in and ask him if there is any reason why there is lipstick on his collar. Maybe there is. Maybe there is a perfectly good explanation, and there's nothing to worry about.

But maybe that woman at the door was telling me the truth.

Maybe my husband has been up to things that he shouldn't have been behind my back.

I grit my teeth and tell myself to not get too emotional or worked up until I have spoken to him. But that's easier said than done, and I decide to take out my phone to give him a call and see where he is. Hopefully he has left his office now and is almost home, so I don't have too long to wait to have this conversation. I could ask him about the lipstick over the phone, but I want to be able to see his face when I do.

I want to see his reaction to my discovery.

I hold my mobile to my ear as I wait for him to pick up but he doesn't, so my call goes to voicemail. I hang up before leaving a message and decide to type out a quick text instead.

What time will you be home?

Then I put my phone down on top of the washing machine beside the incriminating item of clothing and take a deep breath.

I'm going to have to be patient.

But it doesn't mean I have to be sober.

Walking into the kitchen, I go into the fridge and take out a small can of vodka and tonic. I like these little cans because they're not too big and they're much easier than having to pour the drink myself. All I have to do is crack the lid open and take a sip.

The alcohol is refreshing as it should be on a Friday night after what has been an eventful week. It was Monday when I almost died at work, so I think this drink is well earned, regardless of what I have discovered tonight. It's now almost been a week since that woman knocked on my front door, and I'd like to say that the time has flown since then, but it hasn't. Every day has just been a dreary drag and filled with all sorts of worries and doubts about what she said to me. It's funny to think that this time last week, I was a happy woman without a care in the world. I certainly didn't have anything to worry about regarding my husband anyway. But all that has changed now.

Last Friday, I was drinking for fun.

But this Friday, I am drinking to forget.

I'm halfway through the can before I hear the sound of my phone vibrating on the top of the washing machine where I left it. I head back into the utility room to pick it up, and as I do, I see Sam's name on the screen.

'Hi,' I say as I answer the call before taking another sip of my rapidly disappearing drink.

'Hey. Is everything okay? Sorry I missed your call.'

'Yeah, it's fine. Did you get my text?'

'Yeah, I'll be home soon. Just finishing up a few things at the office.'

'Okay.'

'Dinner's at eight tonight, right?'

'Yeah.'

'Great. I'll be home as quick as I can. See you soon. Love you.'

I hesitate slightly before replying.

'Love you too.'

The line goes dead, and I lower my phone before taking another swig from my can. I've almost finished it now, and I'm on my way to the fridge to get another one before I even realise what I'm doing. But screw it. I'm not going to be drunk off a couple of small cans of vodka and tonic. They don't even put that much alcohol in these things anyway.

Opening the second can, I think about Sam and the awkward question I am going to have to ask him when he gets home. It's a shame that we are going to have to start the weekend that way but it has to be done. I have to find out where that lipstick came from.

I just hope he has a good answer for me.

If not, this definitely won't be the last drink that I'll be having tonight.

17

SAM

I could tell that Rebecca had been drinking from the second that I walked through the front door and laid eyes on her. She didn't have a glass in her hand, but she had that look in her eyes that she always gets when she's had alcohol. Like she's a little hazy. She's not drunk by any means. She usually starts swaying and singing when she gets that far along. But she is definitely tipsy, and I'm surprised because I've never known her to be one to drink alone. Sure, it's Friday night, and we have dinner plans with friends, so I could understand her having one or two. But one or two wouldn't be enough to give her that look in her eyes.

She's definitely had more than that.

But why?

'Hey. Good day?' I ask her as I walk over to her and try to get a better read on the situation.

'Yeah. Not bad. You?'

Rebecca's response is a casual one. Does she not want me to know that she has been drinking without me? She didn't slur her words, so maybe she thinks she has gotten away with it. But she can't hide that look in her eyes.

'Work was fine. The usual. Too many meetings. Not enough actual work being done.'

I lean in to give my wife a kiss, and I'm expecting to smell or perhaps even taste the alcohol on her lips, but I don't get the chance to.

That's because she pulls away from me.

'Is everything okay?' I ask, wondering why she has just rejected me for the first time since we have been together.

'You tell me,' Rebecca replies, and that's when she walks into the utility room.

I have no idea what she is doing, but I don't have to wait too long to find out. A few seconds later and she returns to the kitchen with one of my white work shirts in her hands. Then she tosses it to me, and I manage to catch it, although I'm not sure why we are playing catch with my clothes.

'What?' I ask.

'Look at it,' she tells me, and I do as I'm told, but the shirt looks pretty normal to me.

'What's wrong with it?'

'Check the collar.'

I do, and that's when I notice the red smear across it. That's weird. I have no idea what it is, and I definitely hadn't noticed it when I was wearing it a day or two ago.

'What is that?' I ask as I have a go at wiping it off, but it's already pretty well rubbed in and doesn't come off despite my best efforts.

'It's lipstick.'

'Lipstick?'

I have another go at wiping it but no good. I hope it will come out in the washing machine, but maybe it's okay because it's on the underside of the collar so that nobody has to see it. I guess that's how I missed it when I put it on the other day. But how did it get under there?

'It's definitely lipstick,' Rebecca tells me as if to clear up any doubt I might have had. But I'm not arguing. If she says it's lipstick, I guess it's lipstick.

'How did you get lipstick on it?' I ask her, not that I'm blaming her. I'm just confused as to why she is making a big deal about it. Maybe she's annoyed because this is a relatively new shirt, and she thinks it might be ruined now. But it's not, and besides, it's not as if it's expensive.

'It's not mine!'

'What?'

'I said it's not my lipstick. I don't have a shade like that, and even if I did, I haven't been anywhere near any of your shirts with it.'

'You must have done. How else did it get on here?'

'You tell me.'

I don't like the way Rebecca said that, and now I realise what's going on here.

She thinks this lipstick belongs to another woman.

'Look, I don't know how I got lipstick on my collar, but I can assure you that it's not from some woman.'

'Then how did it get there? Have you been wearing lipstick?'

'Don't be stupid.'

'Am I being stupid right now? Am I stupid for believing you instead of that woman the other night?'

'Hey! That's enough!'

I hate to raise my voice at my wife, but I had to do something. I'm not going to stand here in my own home and be accused of being unfaithful.

'What is going on here?' I ask, throwing the shirt onto the kitchen table and taking a few steps towards Rebecca. 'I thought we'd agreed that what happened last Saturday was just an unpleasant incident and that it didn't mean anything.'

'We did. But that was before I found another woman's lipstick on your clothes.'

I look into my wife's eyes, the eyes that are clouded by alcohol, and I have to believe that her current state of inebriation is not going to do me any favours as I try to talk this through rationally.

'Have you been drinking?' I ask, even though I know the answer. I just want to see if she lies to me.

'Yes. I've had a few drinks.'

'How many?'

'I don't know. Who cares? Just tell me how that lipstick got on your shirt!'

'I have no idea, Rebecca!'

'You're lying to me!'

We're both shouting now, and that's never a good sign. That's why I pause for breath and try to figure out how to stop this argument from escalating further.

'Do you want me to cancel tonight? You're obviously not in the right frame of mind, and I'm not really in the mood for it now either if I'm honest.'

'No, I'm not cancelling. I want to go and see my friend. I also want my husband to tell me the truth!'

'About what?'

'About everything! The woman at the door! The lipstick. What's going on?'

'Nothing is going on!'

'I don't believe you!'

There. She's said it. Now I know. My wife no longer trusts me. And why? Because of some lying bitch on our doorstep last week and a random lipstick stain which I genuinely have no idea about how it came to be there.

'I don't know what to say to you,' I tell Rebecca as I sink into a chair. 'I've never lied to you, and I've certainly never cheated on you. I don't know what else I can do.'

'You can explain things.'

'How can I explain something if I don't understand it?'

'You need to do better than that!'

'I can't!'

Rebecca shakes her head and storms past me, where I presume she is on her way out of the kitchen. But she isn't. She is going back to the fridge for another drink. I watch her crack the lid open on a can of vodka and tonic, which I guess is her drink of choice tonight, and she takes a long gulp before coming up for air.

‘I’m not going out with you if you’re going to be like this,’ I tell her, being honest like I always am. Maybe that’s my problem.

Maybe I should start lying.

‘You’re coming out because I’m not cancelling, and I’m not explaining why you couldn’t make it. So get yourself ready. But don’t think I’ve forgotten about this. I won’t forget about it until you tell me the truth.’

With that, Rebecca walks out of the room, taking her drink and her bad mood upstairs, where she is going to get ready for our dinner this evening. It’s a double date, but the idea is almost laughable right now because we are at war, so I hardly feel like playing happy couples with other people.

What should I do?

I guess I’ll take a leaf out of Rebecca’s book and have a look in the fridge.

If she’s drinking tonight, so am I.

18

REBECCA

I should have cancelled this dinner. I should have known it was going to be a disaster ever since the argument when Sam got home. But I foolishly kept the booking, and now I'm sitting in this restaurant opposite my best friend and her boyfriend while my husband sits beside me stewing in his bad mood. I'm not the only one who's been drinking a little too much tonight. Sam had a few beers after I left him in the kitchen. I knew that when I came down an hour later and saw him sitting there with the empty cans in front of him.

Now we're both drunk, and we're both mad at each other.

We've somehow got to get through this meal without the people opposite us realising that.

While my marriage might be lacking right now, at least this restaurant is nice. It's an Italian, and I've never been here before, but I've heard good things. So far, those things have been true. The service has been exquisite, the food has been divine, and the atmosphere in this room is warm. The company is good too. My best friend is called Ally, and her boyfriend's name is Phil. I've been friends with her since school, and she's been dating him since last summer. That's only a few months, but by Ally's standards, that's a long time. It's also a good sign that she is bringing Phil on a double date with us because it must mean that she is serious about this guy. And I can see why she might be. From what I can tell so far, Phil is a friendly and charming man who looks dashing in his smart blue shirt. But apparently, he's not the only one.

'I like your shirt, Sam,' Ally says. 'It's very dapper.'

'Thanks,' Sam replies before taking a large glug from his pint glass. He's going to need another drink soon if he keeps going like that, but I think that is the plan. I really hope he doesn't get too drunk tonight and do something embarrassing, but then I'm in no position to criticise. I've been knocking the drinks back as well, and we're only on our starter. There's a long way to go in this meal yet, but it'll be over quickly if hubby and I keep drinking like fish.

'So, how's your week been?' Ally asks me. 'Any funny things happen on site?'

'Just the usual,' I reply.

'Ally tells me you're an engineer,' Phil says, looking impressed. 'That sounds cool.'

'I get to wear a bright green jacket and boss some men around on a building site. It could be worse, I suppose.'

Phil laughs at my joke, and Ally does the same. But Sam doesn't. He just picks up his pint glass again.

'I can't imagine you working on a building site,' Phil says to Ally. 'But I'd love to see it.'

'Hey!' she cries, playfully hitting her partner on the arm. 'I'd look great in a hard hat and boots, I'll have you know!'

Phil gives her a wink, and I smile because it's clear that these two are very happy together, although I already knew that from what Ally has been telling me over these last few months. She really likes this guy, and while I'm not getting carried away, I have a feeling she thinks he might be the one.

It's about time she found 'the one'.

She's spent the last ten years trying almost every other 'one' in town.

I'm happy for my friend, but I'm also a little sad because seeing the pair of them like this is reminding me how bad things are in my relationship right now. In normal circumstances, Sam and I would be teasing each other and having a laugh too, but these are not normal circumstances.

I don't know what's going on anymore. I had really been hoping that he was going to give me a plausible explanation as to why there was lipstick on his shirt collar earlier, but he wasn't able to manage it. He didn't even give me an explanation of any sort, which only served to make me angrier, as well as more anxious.

That makes two things that he hasn't been able to explain now. The woman at the door and the lipstick. Am I right to be concerned? Should I have been more understanding? Or should I have cancelled this meal and told him that he had to get out of the house unless he gave me a better explanation about the troubling events?

I don't know. I've never had to deal with something like this before. I've had relationships before Sam, but they ended because we drifted apart, not because anybody strayed. It wasn't something that I ever spent much time worrying about then, and I hadn't expected to start worrying about it when I got married either. Cheating, lying and secrets are things that happen between couples on TV shows I watch, not things that happen in my marriage. But unlike those TV shows, this can't be sorted out by a scriptwriter who can make things up as they go along. This is real life. This is my life. So why do I feel like I'm losing control of it?

'So what kind of projects do you work on?' Phil asks me, clearly very keen on what I do for a living. But I'm happy to chat about it. It's not as if my husband has been a font of conversation since we sat down at this table.

'All sorts, really. We're currently building a new drainage system for excess stormwater to run off into.'

'Cool,' Phil says, and I'm not sure if he really means it, but I appreciate the effort.

'It's not that cool,' Sam mumbles before finishing his pint and looking around for the waiter so he can order another one.

'What?' I say, unsure what he means.

'I said it's not that cool. You almost died the other day.'

'You what?' Ally cries, almost knocking her wine over as she sits forward in concern.

'I didn't almost die,' I say, batting the air and trying to play it down, mainly because I don't want to concern my friend, nor do I want everybody to know what happened on site last Monday. But it seems like Sam does.

'Yes, you did. You walked behind an excavator when it was reversing, and you would have been squashed if you hadn't been pulled out of the way.'

'Oh my gosh, Rebecca! Really?'

I glare at my husband, annoyed that he has told this story because I didn't want anybody outside of him or my work colleagues knowing about it. The last thing I need is the story getting back to my parents because they'll only worry, and I know they already feel anxious about me spending my time on building sites. They'd be much happier if I worked in a warm, cosy office somewhere away from big machines and burly men, but I wouldn't be, which is why I chose the career I did. But it's not helping my cause having Sam telling people how I almost died in my dangerous workplace.

'It sounds worse than it was,' I try, but Ally isn't buying it because she knows me well enough to tell when I'm playing something down.

'I'm so glad you're okay. How did it happen?'

'You don't want to know, trust me,' Sam says with a chuckle that irritates me. He only does that chuckle when he is drunk and in a mischievous mood, but the mischief on his mind tonight is not of the fun variety.

'What happened?' Ally asks again, taking the bait that Sam has given her.

'It's nothing. Seriously,' I try, but Sam is happy to carry on the conversation even if I'm not.

'It's because she was thinking about me and some other woman and wondering if I had cheated on her,' he says, sending the atmosphere at this table in a very unpleasant direction.

Poor Phil has no idea what to say to that, but he's not the only one. Ally is looking at me like she can't believe what she has just heard.

'What's he talking about?' she asks me.

'It doesn't matter,' I say, but Sam just gives that chuckle again.

'Of course it matters,' he tells the table. 'My wife thinks I'm cheating on her, which I'm not, by the way. But she doesn't believe me, and I'm not sure what else I can do. Phil, have you got any tips to help a guy out?'

I glare at my husband while he just sits there with a stupid grin on his face. Phil and Ally don't know what to say or where to look, and it's only the arrival of the waiter at our table that cuts through the tension and gives us all something else to focus on for the time being.

'Another pint, please, my good man,' Sam says. 'Make that two, actually. You look like you could do with another one, Phil.'

Phil nods his head. He definitely looks like he could do with another drink. Ally says she wants another one too, and now everyone is looking at me to see what I am going to order.

But what I want isn't on the menu.

What I want is the truth from my husband.

How do I ask the waiter for that?

19

SAM

Well, that meal was a shambles. To be fair, I played a part in that, but I'm not the only one to blame. Rebecca contributed to the disastrous dinner too, and I'd feel sorry for Ally and Phil if I wasn't feeling so sorry for myself. I accept that I had too much to drink tonight but can anyone blame me? I feel like I'm not in control of my life lately, and I had to do something to make myself feel like I was, even if that thing was to drink too much and let off some steam.

But did I go too far? Possibly. I regret mentioning Rebecca's near-miss on site the other day to her best friend. There was no need to bring that up and cause undue concern and worry, and Ally looked very troubled when she heard about it. I also regret going one step further a few moments after that and explaining why Rebecca had been so distracted on site.

I told Ally and Phil that Rebecca thinks that I'm cheating on her.

Poor Phil. He seemed like a good guy, and tonight was supposed to be about us meeting him, but in the end, it turned out to be all about us while he was just a witness in a car crash of a meal. He was probably a little nervous about meeting his partner's best friend and husband for the first time and possibly worried about saying or doing something wrong. But he need not have been so concerned. I did everything wrong for him. I knew I'd gone too far when Rebecca got up from the table and stormed off across the restaurant, leaving me sitting there awkwardly with Ally and Phil until Ally got up and went after her friend. That just left us two guys, and neither of us really knew what to say then. I tried to make a joke about women and how hard it can be to keep them happy, but poor Phil wasn't really in the mood for jokes, and he just stared hopelessly in the direction of where Ally had gone, no doubt praying that she would come back soon and extricate him from the uncomfortable meal.

In the end, I apologised to Phil and stood up before also apologising to the waiter who had just brought me a fresh pint of lager before making my way out to try and find my wife.

Rebecca was outside the restaurant crying into Ally's shoulder when I found her. It takes a brave man to approach his wife when she is upset with him, but it takes an even braver man to do so when her best friend is present too. But I was drunk, so bravery was in my armoury on that occasion, or at least false courage was.

I had tried to calm Rebecca down as well as tell Ally that this was all one big misunderstanding and that I wasn't cheating on my wife. Of course, Ally took Rebecca's side. She had to. It was her duty as her best friend to do so. I get that. But I was persistent and refused to go back inside the restaurant until I was able to speak with my wife alone, and thankfully, Rebecca gave me that opportunity in the end. She had told Ally that she was okay, even though the mascara running down her cheeks told a different story, and the friend had gone back inside, leaving the pair of us to try and have an adult conversation.

That wasn't an easy thing to do considering that we were both drunk and standing in a public place, but I did my best by going first. I apologised to Rebecca for spilling our secrets, and I apologised for drinking too much and making things worse. I told her that I had been out of order at the table and shouldn't have told Ally and Phil those personal things. They were secrets, and they were for her to share with her friend, not me. And then I ended by sharing a secret of my own.

I told Rebecca that I had contacted a private investigator to try and find out who that woman at the door was.

I'm not sure what kind of reaction I had been hoping to get from my wife by giving her that news. Maybe I had hoped that it would prove to her how innocent I was and how determined I am to get to the bottom of all the weird things that have been going on lately. But if that's what I had hoped to happen, I was wrong. *Again.* Rebecca erupted at me as soon as I mentioned the PI. She took it really badly and made out like I was doing anything to avoid coming clean and telling her the truth. She begged me to just be honest with her and admit to whatever I had been doing so she could at least make a decision based on all the facts.

It was clear then that my wife fully believes that I have cheated on her.

But I couldn't admit to something that I hadn't done. I'm innocent, at least as far as being a faithful husband goes. That's why I was adamant when I again told her that I had done nothing wrong and that I didn't know how many times I was going to have to say it. But she wasn't having any of it, and maybe it was the alcohol, or maybe it was just because she was sick of all the fighting, but she told me that she needed a break.

She told me that she didn't want me to stay at home tonight.

That was hard to hear, and it was even harder when she moved away from me as I tried to console her and change her mind. But Rebecca was adamant. She needed some space to think. She needed time to do that thinking.

Basically, she needed me out.

What choice did I have? Stand and continue a drunken argument outside a restaurant or listen to what she wanted and go home and get my toothbrush. I decided to do the latter, and that's why I'm now sitting here, in this rubbish hotel room that I have been forced to book for the night so my wife can have that space and time that she needs. I haven't brought much with me because I'm hoping this will be the only night that I have to stay here, but I guess I'll find out about that in the morning. Of course, I could have gone to a friend's place, but that would have meant having to explain to them why my wife wasn't letting me stay in her bed at the moment, and I couldn't be doing with that. This is between the two of us. That's why I regret that Ally and

Phil know all about our troubles now. But it's too late to put that cat back in the bag as far as they are concerned.

I don't know if Rebecca went and finished the meal with her best friend or not because I just left the restaurant and went home, throwing a few things into a bag and then taking a taxi to the nearest hotel. Now I'm lying on my rented bed for the night, sipping from a can of warm lager that I picked up down in the hotel bar just before they closed for the night. I should go to sleep, or at least stop drinking and start sobering up so I'm ready for tomorrow, but right now, all I want to do is keep drowning my sorrows.

I grimace at the warm alcohol as it slips down my throat and wish that it was ice-cold like it was meant to be consumed, but I'm wishing for a lot of things recently, and none of them are coming true. I wish that Rebecca believed me. I wish that I was still at home. I wish I knew why there had been lipstick on my shirt collar. And I wish that I knew who that woman at the door was and why she had planted that seed of doubt in my wife's mind.

That's when I remember that I haven't checked my personal emails for a while, so I don't know if that PI has got back to me yet. Opening up the app on my phone, I keep sipping my sickly drink as my new emails pop up.

That's when I see it.

The private investigator has replied.

I still don't know if this person is a man or a woman, but that doesn't matter right now. All that matters is that they are willing to meet me to see if they can help me. They ask for a suitable time for this meeting to take place. Can I do midday tomorrow at the cafe on Harvey Street?

I look around the pokey hotel room and at the small pile of my belongings that I took from my house. I hardly have much else going on in my life, do I? That's why I quickly email back and tell the PI that noon tomorrow is fine.

Then I finish my can of warm lager, but I decide not to open the second one.

I'm going to try and get some sleep. I now have a big day tomorrow.

Not only am I going to have to try and get back into my house and fight for my marriage, but I'm also meeting the person who might be able to prove my innocence.

I really hope this PI is as good as their website says they are.

I really hope they can help me find out who that woman at the door was.

20

THE WOMAN

The most important thing that enables me to keep doing what I'm doing is that people never find out who I really am. I use a fake name with all my clients, as well as regularly dye my hair different colours and wear all sorts of different types of clothing, so I'm not recognised or remembered. I also make sure that I work all over the country and not just in one area, increasing my chances of continuing to go undetected.

I don't believe that what I do is illegal. Knocking on a door and telling a lie isn't a crime as far as I know, but I'd rather not have to find out for sure. That's why I need to make sure I avoid any uncomfortable conversations with police officers who might be responding to reports of a woman going around ruining people's marriages.

But it's not just the police that I'm worried about. It's the targets themselves. Those husbands and wives who I am toying with for the benefit of my clients. I don't want to ever come face to face with any of them after that first night when I have paid them a visit. I have the element of surprise on my side when I first knock on their door, and that is what allows me to say my piece and leave before they have a chance to do anything. But if I was to see them again then they would be more prepared, and I can't be having that.

I have no idea what some of those people would do if they got the chance.

Angry husbands or wives, people who had done nothing wrong but had lost their partners thanks to me and my lies. They may get violent with me. They may even try and kill me. I couldn't really blame them for hating me. I'd hate me too if I was an innocent wife who had lost her husband because of a lie and a few strategically placed 'clues.'

That is why I must remain anonymous.

It could literally be a matter of life or death.

But I also have to stay busy because this is a business I'm running, and I'm only as good as my last job. That's why I'm back to work again today dealing with a new client. I'm in Bristol, and I've just had a meeting with a lovely young woman called Zara. She has told me all about her problem, and it's a very familiar one.

She is in love with a man who has a wife.

Zara gave me the man's name, the explanation of how she met him at her weekly gym class and a very impassioned description of why she likes him so much. He's funny, he's smart, he's handsome. All the usual things that can make a woman drawn to a man. But he's also loyal. Zara knows as much because she made a pass at him a month ago while they were together in the corner of a crowded bar after their class went for post-exercise drinks. He had politely turned her down based on the fact that he was married, which was commendable, as well as frustrating. Zara had apologised for her behaviour, afraid that he would hate her for trying something with him, but he had been far too polite to do that, and the pair remained friends, which was good news for my client in one way, but in another way, it was torture.

Zara wanted him.

And she heard that I had ways of potentially making that happen.

I do all my advertising online, but I'm not on social media or anything like that. I simply browse message boards and forums, reading about people who are posting on subjects like unrequited love and what it feels like to find somebody perfect only to have been beaten to them by somebody else. I would sit and read these posts, as well as the comments beneath them from strangers offering their advice.

"Forget about him. You're not meant to be together."

"She's not worth it. There's someone else out there for you."

"Unrequited love is the worst. I'm going through the same thing too. I wish I could help."

It seemed like this was a big problem in society, but more importantly, it seemed like there was nobody out there who was solving it. The advice of "move on and forget about them" was not very helpful to somebody in love. They didn't want to move on. They wanted to be happy.

And to be happy, they needed the other person.

Having seen this 'gap in the market', I had begun to drop myself into these online conversations and provide my own pearls of wisdom. But instead of letting people down gently with token platitudes, I made it clear that there was another option.

I said that the problem was the other man or woman that the subjects were married to.

If they were out of the equation, anything could happen.

It started with one client, as all businesses do. A woman sent me a private message on one of the forums after seeing my group posts, and she asked me what I meant by them. That was when I told her that I had conceived a system that gave people like her a chance with the person they wanted to be with.

I started out by only charging a little. I wasn't entirely sure if it was going to work on demand, after all. But it did. I knew I had something when I got a message from that same woman a few months later telling me that she was now dating the man she desired after he had left his wife due to accusations of cheating levelled against her by me.

My system worked.

It needed ironing out, but it worked.

Thus, my business was born.

But I already knew that because I had tried it before that first customer. I had tried it in my personal life. How do you think I came to be online browsing forums about unrequited love in the first place?

I knew what it was like to want somebody that I couldn't have.

I also knew the kind of things that needed to be done to get them.

21

REBECCA

It's Saturday night, but this is no longer my favourite night of the week. That's because it doesn't consist of any of the things that it used to. There's no takeaway on the sofa. There's no movie on the TV. And there's no Sam sitting beside me laughing.

There's just me, alone in the house, with nothing to do but worry.

I told my husband that I needed some space last night during our ill-fated meal with Ally and Phil. He was shocked when I told him that, but I had to say it because it's the truth. I do need space. I need to think about things, and I can't do that with him around because it's only making me more confused. Sam assumed it was just going to be a one night thing and that he would be able to come back home today. But I told him that I needed more time than that, which is why he has taken a few more of his things and gone back to his hotel.

Just like me, he is going to be spending Saturday night alone.

At least I assume he is.

Who knows what he will really be up to?

I'm standing by the toaster, waiting for my bread to pop up because this is all I'm having for dinner tonight. I could have got a takeaway even though I'm on my own, but I'm not in the mood for it. I just want to eat enough to keep me going and then climb into bed and close my eyes. This is not what weekends are about, and I hope this is not what they will be like in the future, but for now, I'm on my lonesome, and I have to get on with it. Ally had offered to come around and have a glass of wine with me tonight, offering me support and giving me a chance to get more things off my chest regarding my problems with Sam. But I politely put her off, telling her that I'll see her one night in the week for a catch-up. That's because it might not do me much good to have someone else's input into my affairs at this time.

I need to figure this out for myself.

The bread pops up looking much crisper than it did a minute ago, so I scoop it out of the toaster onto a plate and carry it out of the room, along with my cup of tea. I'm heading for the bedroom where I will eat my meagre meal before turning off the lights and thinking about things under the cover of darkness. I like to believe that I do my best thinking during the night when everything is quiet and still. Let's hope so because I need to come to a decision soon on what I am going to do going forward.

Am I going to let Sam back home and, in effect, say that I believe him when he tells me that the woman at the door and the lipstick on the collar had nothing to do with him?

Or am I going to start trusting my gut instinct which tells me that something is wrong and that my husband might not be the perfect man that I thought he was?

Walking into the bedroom, I put my plate and cup down on the bedside table before getting onto the bed and pulling the duvet up over me. It's not even eight o'clock, and I'm already tucked up for the night, but I don't care. I'm entitled to do what I want after the week I have had. From the woman at the door to the near-miss on site to the lipstick on Sam's shirt and the embarrassing argument in front of my best friend, it's been the week from hell.

If I can't have an early night now, when can I?

I must be hungrier than I thought because I eat the toast in no time, and the tea is gone quickly as well. I think about getting up and making more, but I decide not to bother. Instead, I just reach over for the lamp on the bedside table and turn it off.

Now the bedroom is dark, and I can close my eyes and try and get some rest.

As I lie there alone in my bed with my husband several miles away in a hotel room, I think back over our relationship all the way from when we met to this present day. All the dates, from the first few when we were nervous to the later ones when we were far more comfortable with each other. All the text messages, from the flirty ones in the beginning to the more mundane ones after that when we chatted less about sex and more about who would be home first to put the dinner on. All the conversations we had, from the light-hearted and insignificant to the more serious ones where we discussed deep feelings and our plans for the future.

Then there were all the happy times, like the holidays, the nights out and the Sunday mornings in bed spent wrapped up in each other's arms. There were the sadder times, like when Sam's parents passed away and I had to keep him strong during the funerals as he bravely plodded on with life. And there were the truly magical times, like our wedding day and the honeymoon we went on after when we were both glowing from the occasion and feeling content in the knowledge that we had found our one true partner for life.

But it's not just the old times I'm missing now that things have changed. I feel sad for the future times that might not happen now. Getting older together. Celebrating the progression of our respective careers together. Going on holiday together. Spending Saturday nights in front of the TV together.

Just being together in general.

I can't imagine my life without Sam in it.

I thought he felt the same way as I did. I thought he needed me as much as I needed him. But he can't do. Not if he won't be honest with me. He has to know how that lipstick came to be on his shirt, just like he has to know what that woman was talking about when she came to our door this time last week. These things that have happened can't be random or coincidental. They have to mean something, and maybe it's obvious what that thing is.

They mean that my husband has potentially cheated on me while we have been together.

Sam says it isn't so.

But that woman said otherwise.

I know my husband is determined to find out who she is. He has even told me that he has hired a private investigator to look into her. I would like to know too. I want to know who she is and why she came to my house.

I want to know if it was her lipstick on his shirt.

Even if it was true and she slept with Sam, why did she tell me? To get back at him? If so, why? Did he tell her that he was going to leave me but went back on that vow, leaving her angry and vengeful? Or was she just trying to do me a favour by giving me a warning and letting me know that the man I love isn't as innocent as I think he is?

But I don't know why she would feel like she owes me anything. Perhaps she feels guilty about what she did with a married man. Maybe it was her way of easing her conscience.

I just wish Sam would explain all of this, telling me who that woman was and how there is a perfectly good explanation for her appearance. I also want him to explain the lipstick. Give me some reason to think that it got on his shirt innocently and not because he was getting up close and personal with another woman. But he's so stubborn, and he won't do that. He just keeps telling me that he has done nothing wrong. He even said today that he should be innocent until proven guilty, as if he was some suspect in a crime drama on TV, making the detectives do all the work to bring him down. It was almost as if he was putting the onus on me to prove he had strayed rather than having the onus on him to prove that he hadn't. But there is evidence. The woman. The lipstick. It might not be concrete evidence, but it is still evidence, all the same, so therefore he is a suspect. I just don't want to play the detective. I want him to make it easy for me and come clean.

No more interrogations. Just confess. Tell the truth.

Maybe it will break my heart. Maybe it will be the worst thing to hear. But maybe I have to hear it.

Maybe my marriage is over, and maybe I have been a fool.

Maybe.

It's all maybes, and I don't like them. I want solid, irrefutable facts. How do I get them? Perhaps I should take a leaf out of my husband's book and hire a private investigator.

He has hired one to look into that woman.

Maybe I should hire one to look into him.

How's that for a maybe?

22

SAM

It's been a busy start to the weekend and a very unpredictable one. It began with Rebecca telling me to give her some space on Friday night, and it got even weirder when I sat down in a cafe with a private investigator over a cup of coffee on Saturday lunchtime. But before I attended that meeting, I had to pay a visit to Steve's house in the hope that my neighbour would be able to hand me the footage of the woman that I needed in order to give the PI something to work with.

I'd been anxious when I had knocked on Steve's front door and not just because I needed a favour from him. It was because I was so close to my own house, the house I had been told that I wasn't welcome at for the time being. I'd been nervous about Rebecca looking out of the window and seeing me there in case she thought I was loitering around, which is a ridiculous thing to worry about because why should I not be allowed to loiter around near my own home if I wanted to? But I didn't see Rebecca at the window, and I was able to get into Steve's house when he opened the door and begrudgingly agreed to give me the footage of the woman.

With that evidence in my possession, I was able to attend the lunchtime meeting with the PI who had responded to my email, and that was where my crazy week got even crazier. I'm not sure what I had been expecting when I turned up to meet the PI for the first time. Someone in a long coat and hat perhaps, with dark sunglasses covering their eyes and a shifty demeanour as they went about their business hoping that nobody would recognise them? I certainly hadn't been expecting what I got, which was a mousey-haired middle-aged woman who looked more like a librarian than a private investigator.

I knew she was the person I was supposed to meet because she had sent me a text message just before our scheduled meeting time telling me that there would be a red handbag on one of the tables in the cafe, which would be how I was to know where to sit. I had walked into the cafe at noon and seen the red handbag, as well as the woman sitting in front of it, and that was how our meeting had begun.

She told me that her name was Erica, but I had no way of knowing if it was her real name or not because I wasn't going to ask her for I.D. It could have been a pseudonym to keep her real identity a secret, or she could have been perfectly honest. Her job wasn't illegal, so she had no reason to be secretive, but the success of her job did lend itself to being discreet, so who knows? Maybe she was being honest with me, or maybe she was not. But it didn't matter. The important thing was that I was as open and honest with her as possible as I told her my problem and how I hoped that she could solve it for me.

I told her about the woman at the door and the lie she spoke to my wife that I wasn't able to explain. I told her about the footage my neighbour had of the woman as she walked away from our house that night. And I told her that my wife was now paranoid about whether or not I had been cheating on her and that things had come to a head after the discovery of some lipstick on my shirt, which I couldn't explain either, so I was now staying in a hotel to give her a break.

It felt weird to be talking about myself so openly to a complete stranger, but I did my best to give Erica as clear a picture as possible about what has happened to me because that would be the best way that she might be able to help. The PI had recorded everything I had said on a tape recorder that had sat in the middle of the table between us, and while I wasn't sure how good the sound quality would be considering we were sat in the middle of a busy cafe, I had to assume she knew what she was doing. I certainly hoped she did when she gave me her fee a few minutes later.

Erica wanted me to give her £1000 if she was successful with tracking down this mystery woman.

I had initially baulked at the hefty figure she had quoted me and made a comment about how I might have to do some "shopping around" to see if I could find a PI that wasn't quite as pricey. But Erica had assured me that her fee was more than fair and actually quite cheap considering how much work she was going to have to do in finding the woman based on all I had given her to go on.

I had sipped my coffee and deliberated over my decision for a few minutes, but in the end, I decided to go for it because what did I have to lose? I only had to pay Erica if she found this woman, and if she did that then it was potentially going to save my marriage, so it would be money well spent. The other option was not to spend the money and keep paying for a damn hotel room while my wife kept doubting me and thinking I had been up to no good behind her back.

My meeting with Erica had ended when the PI had taken the footage from Steve's CCTV camera and told me that she would be in touch if and when she had something that could help. I had asked her how long that was likely to be, but she couldn't give me a definite answer. She told me that in her line of work, it was difficult to put deadlines on things, and I suppose I can understand that. But I did ask her what she was planning to do to start tracking the woman down, although she didn't tell me. She just said she had her methods and they had worked before, so she was confident that they would work again. And on that mysterious note, she had turned and walked away out of the coffee shop, leaving me to wonder what the hell she was going to do at my expense.

After the covert meeting had ended, I had called round at my house to pick up a few more things to keep me going in my new life as an estranged husband living out of a hotel room. Rebecca had been home, but she hadn't been very chatty and not at all engaging when I had tried to get her to sit down and give me another chance to plead my innocence. She said she still needed more time and that unless I could give her answers about the woman and the lipstick, I would need to make myself comfortable at that hotel.

I had brought up the meeting with the PI and hoped that might go some way to proving how serious I was about uncovering the truth. I even told her that I was willing to spend £1000 if necessary to find out who that woman was and why she had lied. Rebecca had seemed a little shocked by that price tag, as I had been the first time that I had heard it, but she still hadn't accepted that I was innocent in all of this. If she had done then I would have been at home now lying on my own bed instead of on this one right here. The mattress is lumpy, the pillow is as flat as a pancake, and it really isn't worth the £47 a night that I'm paying for the privilege of sleeping on it. But it's very cheap, and that's important because I need to save all the money I can so I can pay the PI to get me out of here and back in my house where I belong.

Do I feel betrayed that Rebecca doesn't believe me? Yes, it would be impossible not to feel hurt about it. She should trust me implicitly, just like I trust her. But I understand that it's not easy. I have tried to put myself in her position and imagine what I would have felt like if some guy turned up at our house and told me that he had slept with Rebecca a month ago. Would I have believed him or her? And what would have happened if I had found something else to make me concerned a few days later as Rebecca did with the lipstick on my collar?

Maybe I would have believed her. Or maybe I would have needed some time too.

This is a rubbish situation, but because I'm innocent, I'm able to cling to the belief that everything will be okay in the end. The truth will come out, and I have nothing to hide.

Nothing at all.

So why do I feel like I can't relax?

23

REBECCA

I slept poorly last night, which was to be expected, I suppose. But instead of moping around the house all day wasting away my Sunday, I decided to give Ally a text and see if she was free to go for a walk. I was glad to hear that she was and now I'm standing in the large park near my house waiting for her to turn up.

It's a bright and breezy morning, suggesting that the worst of winter is behind us in this country and that warmer days are ahead. I certainly hope so because I'm not a fan of the cold, and I hate when it goes dark while I'm still sitting at work. I have no idea how those people in Scandinavia cope where they live in almost permanent darkness for half of the year, but I'm grateful that while the English climate is bad, it's not that bad. The speck of blue sky peeping through the fluffy white clouds overhead tells me that.

Better days are ahead, at least weather-wise anyway.

It remains to be seen if better days are ahead in my personal life.

I spot Ally walking towards me along the path that runs beside the lake, and I set off in her direction, shortening the time that it will take her to get to me. It's nice to be out here in the fresh air beside the water, and the lake is typically busy with a few sailing boats out there as well as a couple of canoeists who look like they're having fun as they paddle around and get some exercise. But I'll stick to the footpath today. I find it much more enjoyable to watch people sailing and canoeing than to actually do those things myself.

'Hey,' I say as I reach Ally, and she gives me a smile and a warm hug before asking if I'm okay.

'Yeah, I'm fine,' I tell her before pointing towards the path that leads up the hill, suggesting that we give that route a go today.

'So, what's the latest?' my friend asks me as we begin climbing the hill, wasting no time in cutting to the chase. But I don't mind that. The whole reason I wanted to see her today is because I needed somebody to talk about my problems with.

'Sam stayed at the hotel again last night,' I tell her, feeling a little embarrassed to be admitting that my marriage is on the ropes right now, but I shouldn't be because Ally won't be judging me. It'll be my husband who is being judged, and that's the beauty of a best friend.

'I can't believe he won't just tell you what's been going on. Surely he knows you aren't going to let him back home until he gives you a reason for that woman and that lipstick.'

'He's still adamant that he hasn't done anything wrong and that he doesn't know who the woman is or why the lipstick got there,' I confirm as we continue to climb the hill.

‘So what are you thinking?’ Ally asks as we pass a young boy on a skateboard. ‘About letting him come home, I mean.’

‘I’m still not sure. I was up most of the night thinking about it, but I have no idea what to do. I never thought I’d have to make a decision like this.’

‘I’m so sorry. You don’t deserve it.’

‘It’s not your fault.’

‘I know. I just feel so bad. I thought you and Sam were the perfect couple, you know? Never argued. Never fought. Certainly never had anything serious happen like this.’

‘Nobody’s perfect,’ I tell my friend as if I’m a wise woman who has lived a hundred years and seen it all. But I’m not a wise woman, and I haven’t seen it all. I’m learning all of this for the first time. I’m figuring it out as I go. That’s why I’m not sure if I’m doing the right thing.

‘What would you do if you were in my situation?’ I ask Ally as we reach a bench near the top of the hill and take a seat to enjoy the view over the lake.

‘I think I’d do the same thing,’ Ally confirms and that makes me feel a little bit better.

‘But what if I’m wrong and he really hasn’t done anything?’

‘What if you’re right and he has?’

That’s a good point and I think about it for a second as I stare out across the water. One of the canoeists has gone away from the main group and seems to be going it alone out there. I guess they don’t mind being by themselves. I wish I felt the same way.

'I don't know what I'll do if things don't get better,' I confess, feeling my eyes watering slightly but wiping them quickly because I don't want Ally to think I'm going to start blubbing in front of her. 'I don't want to be on my own, but I don't know if I can trust him.'

'It's up to him to prove to you that he can be trusted,' Ally tells me, seemingly much surer about things than I am. 'I know you might not want to hear it, but I really don't think a woman would come to somebody's house and say those things unless there was substance to it.'

I know my friend is just giving it to me straight because she is trying to help me and the best way to do that is with brutal honesty, but it still seems harsh to hear it in those terms. Ally must think Sam has cheated on me. But that's easy for her to think. She isn't the one who is married to him, so she doesn't have as much to lose as I do.

'I had an idea,' I say, figuring it might be good to run it past her before I take action on it.

'What's that?'

'I was thinking about getting somebody to follow Sam to see if he is meeting any other women. Like a private investigator.'

'You think they would find something?'

'I don't know. But if he is going behind my back then I can find out.'

Ally's silence makes me a little nervous that I might be going too far with that idea, so I decide to change the subject quickly.

'Anyway, enough about me. What about you and Phil? I'm sorry about the meal the other night. It wasn't the best time for us to meet him.'

'Don't worry about it. He's fine. He's gone fishing today with one of his friends.'

'Fishing. How exciting.'

I roll my eyes and Ally laughs. That's one boring hobby that Sam never had. But maybe it would have been better if he did. Better than getting another woman's lipstick on his collar anyway.

'Yeah, he asked me if I wanted to go with him last week, but I politely declined.'

'I can't imagine you fishing.'

'I know, right? I'd be asleep after five minutes.'

I laugh as I look back towards the lake and see the solitary canoe joining up again with the other members of the group. Maybe that canoeist decided it's better to be together than alone. Maybe I'm realising the same thing.

'I want to tell him to come home,' I say, nodding my head as if to convince myself. 'I don't want to get an investigator and behave like a paranoid wife who doesn't trust her husband. I just don't want to get hurt. Do you know what I mean?'

'Of course I do,' Ally tells me, and she puts a reassuring hand on my arm. 'Just take your time and do whatever feels right for you. The ball is in your court. You don't know if Sam has done anything wrong, but you know that you definitely haven't, so you're entitled to take things slowly.'

I smile at my friend and feel reassured by her advice. I'm glad I messaged her about coming to the park today. The sun has really broken through the clouds now, and there's more blue sky visible than there was when I arrived here. It's shaping up to be a sunny Sunday, and everything always looks better in the sunshine.

That's when I decide that I'm going to go and see Sam after this.

Just like that canoeist went off alone but came back in the end, I'm going to do the same. I feel like there is still enough doubt in my mind to give Sam another chance. I'll tell him he can come home, but only on one condition.

It's the condition that nothing else happens to make me doubt him and his commitment to me.

If it does then that is it. We are finished. I'm not going to be a woman who is walked all over. Like Ally said, I have done nothing wrong. He's the one that has some making up to do, not me.

He's the one that's got it all to do to earn back my trust.

24

SAM

It was shaping up to be a very sorry Sunday until I got the phone call from Rebecca telling me that she wanted to see me. I'd thought that the only thing I had to look forward to all day was the Formula 1 race coming on the TV in my hotel room at 5 o'clock, but fortunately, it seems there might be something even brighter on the horizon.

I might get to go home.

Rebecca has asked to meet me in the same pub where we enjoy our regular Sunday Roasts, but I'm not sure if beef and gravy is going to be on the menu today. The most important thing to do is talk, whether that's over good food, good wine or a glass of tap water. I just want things to go back to normal, and I'm hoping that her call to me today is the beginning of that.

I see her sitting at the table in the corner as I enter the pub, so I hurry over and take a seat opposite her, giving her a nervous smile and noticing the glass of white wine sitting in front of her.

'Starting already?' I say, hoping that a light joke might be the best way to break the ice between us.

'Yeah. Are you having anything?'

'I might get a pint,' I say, glancing back at the bar. But it looks busy and I'd rather just get to the bottom of why I'm here without delaying things any longer.

When I turn to look back at Rebecca, it seems like she wants the same thing. Her hand has reached out across the table and is in search of my own.

'Are you okay?' I ask, taking her hand and wondering what this might mean.

'Not really. I miss you.'

'I miss you too,' I say, and I feel the relief flooding through me because it seems like everything is going to be okay.

'Do you understand why I needed this time?' Rebecca asks me, and I nod to show her that I do.

'Of course.'

'It's just the woman and then the lipstick. I don't know what to think.'

'I understand, and it's not your fault. You've done nothing wrong here.'

'And neither have you?'

I know Rebecca still feels unsure about everything, but all I can do is keep doing what I've always done and that is tell the truth.

'I haven't done anything,' I say as I squeeze her hand. 'I promise.'

Rebecca gives me a faint smile before picking up her wine glass and taking a sip. As she does, I rack my brains for something else to say that can make her feel better.

'Look, the PI is doing her best to try and find out who that woman was, and I'm hopeful she'll be able to get us some answers there. As for the lipstick, I genuinely have no idea how it came to be on there, but I swear on my life that I have not been seeing another woman.'

Rebecca studies me, and she seems to believe me because she nods her head.

'Okay,' she says. 'I want you to come home.'

'Thank you.'

'But if anything else happens then that's it,' she warns me. 'I can't keep giving you a pass if you don't give me answers. Do you understand?'

'I do,' I say, and while I'm relieved about the fact that I get to go home, I do feel anxious about the condition that it comes with. That's because I can't guarantee that there won't be anymore troubling events in the future. I had not expected a woman to come to our door and tell Rebecca that I had slept with her, nor had I been expecting there to be lipstick on my shirt, but both those things have happened. The fact that I don't know how or why those things happened means that I can't be sure that they won't happen again, and that is going to lead to a few sleepless nights even when I am back in my own bed. But what can I do? I just have to hope that nothing else happens as well as hoping that the PI finds that woman so I can get to the bottom of all of this. But that remains to be seen. For now, I just have to take things one step at a time.

'The bar looks quieter,' Rebecca says, and I turn around to see that she is right. The queue has died down now, so I stand up to go and order a drink.

'Do you want another one?' I ask her, referring to the almost empty glass of wine on the table.

'Go on then. And get a menu while you're up there. I'm starving.'

I smile as I make my way to the bar, and I place my order with the barmaid before picking up one of the food menus lying nearby. As I flick through it and peruse the appetising options, I feel relieved that I'm now spending my Sunday afternoon doing something a little more normal than what would have been happening if Rebecca hadn't called me. A takeaway for one in a hotel room with F1 on the TV is hardly my idea of fun because I'm not the biggest fan of the sport or eating alone, so it's much better to be in this busy pub preparing to order a meal with my wife.

These last few days have been a glimpse into what my life would look like if I wasn't married to my beautiful wife. I'd be very bored and very lonely. All my friends have settled down like me, and I'm hardly in the mood for being single again and venturing out onto the dating scene. It's all online apps these days, isn't it? Not for me, thank you very much. I'm perfectly happy with Rebecca, and if I ever had any doubts about married life being the right thing for me then they have been put to bed this weekend after spending most of it on my own without Rebecca by my side.

The barmaid hands me the two drinks and tells me that she will send somebody over to my table in a few minutes to take our food order, so I thank her and carry the beverages back over to where my wife is waiting. She looks much happier now than she did the last time we were out together, which was Friday night at the meal with Ally and Phil that we should definitely have postponed because we were both far too drunk and far too grumpy to be socialising.

I hope this is the start of things returning to how they used to be between us again.

Nights in front of the TV. Takeaway. Roast dinners.

Laughter. Love.

Happiness.

But as I reach the table and place the two drinks down onto it, I'm aware that there will always be a cloud hanging over us. It will be there until I can explain to Rebecca who that woman was and why she was lying. But I need the private investigator to come up trumps for me if I am going to be able to do that. As I take my seat and pull my phone from my pocket, I make a quick check on my text messages and emails on the off chance that the PI has contacted me and given me some good news. But there's nothing from her yet. It's still early days, and it is a Sunday, I suppose. I wonder if Erica has the day off. Do PI's take days off? I guess so. They're still normal people, even if they do a slightly abnormal job.

Putting my phone away, I smile at Rebecca as she picks up the menu and has a look through the options, and everything seems okay again in the world.

If only things had stayed like this forever.

Little did I know it then, but everything was about to change in my marriage, and this time, it would be far worse than anything that had happened before.

25

THE WOMAN

Sundays are always a slow day for me. I guess they are for anybody who is by themselves. But I'm not lonely. This is just the way my life is right now. I could date somebody if I wanted to, but I don't. I'm happy enough being by myself, and it definitely makes things easier for my work. Having a partner would mean having to keep a secret from them as to what it is that I really do for a living. I doubt there are many men who would feel comfortable being in a relationship with a woman who makes her money by breaking married couples up. Besides, if I was with the man who I wanted to be with right now then I wouldn't be doing this job and earning such a good wage.

I only ended up in this life because the man I loved passed away.

His name was Devon, and he was wonderful. I met him at a time in my life when I was just about giving up on men after a string of failed relationships with guys who were either too clingy, too distant or simply too immature. But he was different to those boys. He was a man, and most importantly, he made me feel like a woman.

He was my personal trainer at my local gym, and while it might seem like a cliché to be attracted to a hunky guy who I spent an hour a week with, there was far more to him than muscles and a passion for fitness. He was funny and made me laugh as he put me through my paces every Tuesday evening after I had finished in my office admin job in the city. He was educated, and he informed me about many interesting things regarding diet, exercise and even politics during our time together. And he was charming, complimenting me on several occasions whenever I did something well in the gym and even noticing when I was sporting a new hairstyle or had tried out some new makeup. It wasn't long until I was looking forward to my sessions with Devon and doing my best to impress him with my own brand of wit, knowledge and charm. I had also found myself sneaking a glance at his left hand to make sure that there wasn't a ring that might indicate that he was a married man and therefore unavailable.

But there was no ring, so to me, that meant he was fair game.

That was why I plucked up the courage to ask him out for a drink at the end of one of our sessions when I was feeling particularly confident with all the adrenaline running through my system after a hard workout alongside him. I had been hopeful that he would accept the invitation and felt that he liked me as much as I liked him. But I was wrong. Not about him liking me. I could tell he found me attractive and interesting.

Rather, I was wrong about the fact that he wasn't married.

Devon told me that he did indeed have a wife and that he just didn't wear his ring during his personal training sessions because it made it difficult to grip certain weights and he didn't want to scratch it on any of the equipment. Instead, he kept the ring in his locker and put it back on at the end of every shift. To say I felt stupid was an understatement, and I had apologised to him and tried to make light of it. Fortunately, he took it all in good spirits and didn't let it affect the way he treated me going forward with our future sessions together. But for me, I wasn't able to leave it at that.

I was in love with Devon.

So I had to have him.

The problem was that he was taken, and that was how I had first come to be browsing the internet reading the message boards about other people like me who were in love with people they couldn't have. I saw how I was not alone and that there were so many people out there who felt depressed, lonely and utterly defeated when it came to their love life. It was almost as if we were cursed because we had been fated to fall in love with somebody who could not love us back.

Why hadn't we fallen in love with a single person? Because life didn't work that way. You can't plan love. It just happens. You don't choose who you fall for. You just fall, and it remains to be seen if it's going to be a good thing or a bad thing. For me, it was a bad thing. I fell, and I had no one there to catch me and pick me back up again.

I could have just left it. I could have changed personal trainers or even changed gyms, meaning I never had to see him again. But I didn't because I needed to see him. I craved him. He was the only thing in my life that made me feel alive. So I carried on the sessions, and I carried on loving him even though it was cutting me up inside that he was going home to his wife every night while I was going home alone.

That was when I had an idea, and it was the idea that would change both mine and his life forever.

I decided to follow him home one evening. That was how I found out where he lived. That was how I saw his wife.

And that was where I had the idea to do something about her.

I can't remember the exact moment the idea came to me, but when it did, I had felt an exhilarating rush because I knew that if it worked then it was going to potentially make everything that I wanted come true.

I went back online and posted an advert asking for an attractive and athletic woman who was willing to do one minute's work for me in exchange for £200. Perhaps unsurprisingly, I got quite a few replies, and after asking a few of the women to send me their photos, I selected one and told her to meet me near Devon's house. When she did, I was pleased to see that the woman had been honest in her description of herself and was both attractive and athletic, which was important because I needed her to look like somebody Devon would be interested in. Because she had been honest with me, I was then honest with her. I showed her the £200 and told her what she needed to do to get it.

She had to go and knock on Devon's door and tell his wife that she had slept with him.

The woman had been a little surprised to hear what I wanted her to do, but I had made sure to flash the money again and reminded her that it could be hers if she did what I asked. So the woman agreed. She was to knock on the door, tell the woman who answered it that Devon had been her personal trainer and that they had slept together and that she was telling the wife because she felt guilty about it. Then all she had to do was walk away and she would get the money.

The woman did exactly what I asked of her, and I was happy to give her the money.

Then all I had to do was see what the fallout from her words would be.

It was a few days later, during my weekly gym session with Devon, when I noticed that he was a little quieter and less enthusiastic than normal. I had asked him if everything was okay, and he had tried to let me know that it was, but he had done a bad job of it, and that's when he asked me for my advice. He told me that he had been arguing with his wife, and she was accusing him of something that he didn't do. Did I have any suggestions as to how to make things better? I said that I did. I told him to be a man and go home and assert himself. Tell her the truth and let her know that she had to trust him, or their relationship could never survive.

I told him to do that because I knew that his wife would not be satisfied with something like that. How could she be? There was no way she could ever trust him fully again after what the woman at the door had told him. It was a few nights later, when I was making a check on Devon's house, when I saw him packing his things into the back of the car. He was moving out. His wife had made him leave. She could clearly no longer trust him.

That meant their marriage was doomed.

Of course, I had no idea that my plan was going to work, but it did work and with Devon no longer attached to anybody, I was able to have another go at sparking his interest in me. I again asked him for a drink after one of our classes and he accepted the offer this time. Presumably, it was either that or go back on his own to wherever he was staying. One drink led to several, and by the end of the night, Devon was in my bed.

He ended up spending rather a lot of time in there while he went through the divorce process with his wife.

It had worked. I had snared my dream man. I had turned unrequited love into reciprocated love. I had proven all those people on the forums wrong. I wasn't doomed after falling in love with the wrong person. I was lucky, and I had made it work.

It was one year later, just a few weeks after Devon's divorce had been finalised, when he left my place early one morning to go to the gym. But he never made it. His car was struck by a drunk driver who had veered onto the wrong side of the road, and that was it. Devon was gone.

He would never have been on that particular road at that particular time if he hadn't stayed over at mine. But I couldn't think like that. I had loved him, and I had ensured that his last few months of life had been filled with love. But that didn't change the fact that I was alone again.

I'd lost everything that I'd worked for. I felt helpless. But I had learnt one thing.

I had learnt how to get a person who wasn't available.

I had created a system to test even the strongest of marriages.

All I had to do then was share it with the world.

26

REBECCA

It's nice to no longer be alone in the house after spending most of the weekend on my own. Sam moved back in after we had finished at the pub and he had gone back to the hotel to gather up the few things that he had stored there. He had already paid for that night's stay, but I'm sure he was more than happy to check out early and get back to his own bed. He's lying in that bed right now waiting for me to finish up in the bathroom, and I wonder if he's hoping that we are going to be doing a little more making up when I come to join him under the duvet. I guess we should. It's only natural for a couple to talk things through first before getting physical to show that things are back to normal. But it will be the first time that I have been intimate with my husband since the suspicions of him being unfaithful first surfaced, and I'm not sure how I'm going to feel when we are in the moment.

Will I be fully engaged with him and able to enjoy myself like I used to? Or will my brain be filled with thoughts of that other woman and how Sam might have been intimate with her?

I pick up my electric toothbrush and go to turn it on, but the battery is flat, reminding me that I forgot to put it on charge when it ran out this morning. It's hardly surprising that I forgot to do such a simple task when my mind was filled with more important things. I'll just have to make do with brushing without the battery, using elbow grease instead of electricity to clean off the food and wine I consumed in the pub earlier today.

As I brush my teeth, I stare at my reflection in the mirror and notice how tired I look. It's been a while since I had a good night's sleep, and it's showing. Hopefully, I'll get a good eight hours tonight before work in the morning, but I won't hold my breath. It's not because I might be up late into the night making passionate love to my husband, nor is it because Sam might be snoring loudly when he falls asleep. It's because my mind is at that stage where it's so riddled with doubts and worries that it's impossible to quieten my thoughts and achieve the peace of mind required to drift off into slumber. Even the glasses of wine I consumed today at the pub won't help me much because my mind becomes even more active when I drink alcohol. As I finish up with my teeth and put the toothbrush onto the charger so that it's more useful for me the next time I use it, I get one last glance at my haggard face and think about how 'lucky' Sam is to be getting to spend the night with me.

Walking back into the bedroom, I see him lying on his side of the bed. He has his hands behind his head and looks very much at home, which of course he is, but maybe he looks a little too comfortable considering that he has spent the last two nights in a hotel because of some troubling things that he can't explain. But I'm probably just reading too much into things, and I know it's unhealthy to do that. It's also unfair on Sam as well because if I say that I am trusting him then I can't be judging him or analysing his behaviour when he is just being himself. If he looks comfortable and casual in the bed, it's because he is comfortable and casual, and not because he is feeling smug, or satisfied, or like he has gotten away with doing something that he shouldn't have.

'I think I might have had one too many at the pub,' Sam says to me as I take out my earrings and place them on my dresser table. 'There's nothing like starting the week with a mild hangover.'

I smile as I pick up a hairbrush and start to comb my hair. But Sam is clearly getting impatient for me to come and join him in the bed, and I see him wriggling in the reflection of the dresser table mirror before he tells me to come and join him.

'One minute,' I say, making sure to get my hair in a semi-decent state before I go and lie on my pillow, so it's not got even more knots in it than it's going to have in the morning.

'I've missed you,' Sam tells me, slurring his words slightly, which reinforces what he just told me about potentially having one too many drinks today. But I appreciate the sentiment, even if it is a little cheesy.

'It's only been two nights,' I tell him. 'And you called round yesterday to get some things.'

'I know, but I still missed you.'

I smile and put down my hairbrush before heading over to my chest of drawers.

'What are you doing now?' Sam moans, clearly extremely eager to get his hands on me under that duvet.

'I'm just getting my clothes ready for the morning.'

'Leave it.'

'No, you know that I like to get it done so I won't wake you when I get up.'

'I don't care.'

'It only takes a second.'

Sam lets out a deep sigh, but I carry on with what I'm doing because it really will only take a second. I've gotten into the habit over the years of getting out my clothes for tomorrow the night before. That's because I get up earlier than my husband, sometimes even two hours before him due to how early I have to be on site some mornings, so it's easier for me to do this than to be scrabbling around trying to do it quietly in the dark the next day. I always get out a pair of jeans, a pair of socks and a pair of knickers, as well as some kind of top, although it doesn't really matter so much what the top looks like because it's always covered up by my coat and my hi-viz jacket by the time that I get to the site anyway. I could just leave this until the morning like Sam says, but I'll do it now so that it's done and it's one less thing to have to think about on a Monday morning.

Opening up the second drawer, I take out a top before opening the first drawer and rummaging inside for socks and knickers. I find a pair of black socks, and I place them on top of the chest of drawers with the top before going back into the drawer for the knickers. Any pair will do, I'm not going to be flashing them to anybody after all, and I'm just about to take out a rather large and unflattering pink pair when I notice the red panties in the drawer beside them.

I know instantly that they are not mine because I do not own a single pair of red panties.

Picking them up and holding them out in front of me, I get a better look at them, and it only confirms what I knew. They are definitely not mine. They are very skimpy and very sexy, and they are two things that the underwear in my drawer can never be called.

So if they're not mine, who the hell do they belong to?

I dread the answer, but I have to have it, so I turn around and face my husband in the bed, holding up the pair of mystery knickers in front of me.

'What the hell are these?'

Sam's satisfied expression suddenly becomes more serious.

'What?'

'Who do these belong to?'

'What are you talking about?'

'I'm talking about these!' I say before throwing them at his face.

'Hey!' he cries as he gathers them up and looks at them.

'They're not mine. So who the hell do they belong to?'

'I don't know.'

'You don't know?'

'No!'

'How did they get in here? I sure as hell didn't put them in here!'

'Neither did I!'

'Are they hers?' I ask, almost before I've even had a chance to think the question through.

'Who?'

'Hers! That bitch that turned up on our doorstep last week! Do you they belong to her? Has she been in here?'

'No, of course not!'

'She's been in here, hasn't she! That's how she knew where you lived. That lipstick was hers, and those knickers are hers too!'

'Rebecca, calm down!'

'Get out! I want you gone now!'

'Don't be ridiculous. I've only just come back.'

'I don't care. I can't do this.'

'Just take a second to think this through. If I had been cheating on you then why would I put that woman's underwear in your drawer for you to find?'

'I don't know! You obviously made a mistake!'

'I haven't made a mistake because I've done nothing wrong!'

'Then how did they get here?'

'I have no idea.'

'Is that your answer for everything? The woman at the door. No idea. The lipstick on the shirt. No idea. Knickers in our bedroom. No idea!'

'Rebecca, please, you need to calm down.'

Sam gets out of the bed and tries to come closer to me, but he is still holding the red panties in his hand, and the sight of them is making my blood boil.

'I've been an idiot. I should have listened to that bitch when she told me what you had done. I should never have given you a chance.'

'Something's going on here. Somebody else has put these here.'

He holds up the knickers, but I lash out at them and send them flying away into the corner of the room.

'She put them here!' I say. 'Right after she fucked you in our bed!'

Sam is clearly stunned at my outburst and choice of words, but I'm only saying what I'm thinking. But I need to get away from my cheating rat of a husband, and I need to do it now. But if he won't go and get out of my sight then I will have to go somewhere myself so that I don't have to look at him anymore.

Storming into the bathroom, I slam the door behind me and quickly lock it so that he can't come in after me. I hear him trying the handle before banging on the door, but I ignore it and put the toilet lid down to take a seat on it.

'Rebecca! Open the door!' Sam calls out as he continues to knock, but I'm not planning on letting him anywhere near me.

Not tonight. Maybe not ever.

'Just pack your things again and get out!' I scream back at him.

'I'm not going anywhere until you open this door and let me explain this.'

‘What is there to explain?’ I cry back before I feel my breath catch in my throat and a wave of nausea come over me.

Am I going to be sick? I think I might be, so I quickly get up off the toilet lid and open it up so that I’m prepared just in case.

The reason for my sudden sickness is that I feel like this is going to be the moment when Sam confesses to sleeping with that other woman and, in the process, destroys the whole concept of our marriage as well as the plans I had for the next forty years of my life.

This is it. This is the moment when the truth comes out.

This is the moment when my world comes crumbling down.

Is it any wonder I’m going to be sick?

‘I haven’t cheated on you, Rebecca. I swear.’

Sam’s words through the bathroom door are not a confession. Instead, they are a continuance of the same thing he has been telling me all week. Even now, after the evidence is becoming insurmountable, he still refuses to do me the decency of telling me the truth.

Who does he think I am?

‘Then how did those knickers get in here?’ I scream back at him. ‘Answer me that!’

‘I don’t know,’ he replies.

‘You’re going to have to do better than that!’

‘It’s the truth. I honestly don’t know, but I swear I’ve never seen them before!’

‘I’m sick of you swearing things. I’ve had enough of it. Just go!’

The sickness has passed for the time being, but the tears are coming on strong now, and my eyes start stinging as I take several deep breaths and do my best not to have a nervous breakdown right here on my bathroom floor.

'Rebecca. Please open the door,' Sam tries again.

'Just leave me alone!'

The volume of my voice and the venom in my words comes as a shock to me, but I guess it also comes as a shock to Sam because he stops trying the door handle.

Ten seconds later and I can hear him opening and closing the wardrobe door in the bedroom, which suggests that he is doing as I have asked and is packing up his things to make a return to that hotel. But I'm not going to go out and see him before he leaves. I'm going to stay in here until I hear the front door close behind him. Maybe I'll stay in here all night, kneeling down on the bathroom floor with my arms resting on the toilet seat and my face over the bowl.

Why not?

It's not as if I have anything to come out of here for anymore.

27

SAM

I'm getting a feeling of deja-vu as I stand in this hotel lobby and ask the woman behind the desk to provide me with a keycard so I can access my room. That's because it was only a couple of nights ago when I checked in here after Rebecca had kicked me out the first time. Now I'm checking in again, although technically I'm not because I still have a room booked for tonight after assuming I would need it before my wife and I made up at the pub. But that reconciliation has already broken down again, and here I am, back at the hotel and back to square one.

'Here's your card, sir,' the polite receptionist tells me as she slides the white keycard across the desk towards me.

She can probably see on the system that I already checked out early this afternoon, but she hasn't bothered asking me why I'm back, which is a relief. It's also a relief that my room is still available and they didn't give it to somebody else because that would have been another problem for me and I've already got enough of those. Thankfully, the keycard is back in my hand and that means I can now go up in the elevators and get into my room where I can put my bags down and try and figure out what the hell I'm going to do next.

As I push the button for the fourth floor, my head is throbbing as I try to process what has just happened to me. One second I was lying in bed waiting for my wife to come and join me and the next, I was banging on the bathroom door after she had locked herself in after finding some underwear in her drawer that didn't belong to her. I can see how that might look bad, but I genuinely have no idea how that item of clothing came to be there.

Just like the lipstick.

And just like the woman at the door.

It's clear that there is a pattern here, but it's not one that covers me in any glory. There's only so many times that I can tell Rebecca that I don't know what is going on before she has a right to call me a liar and a cheat, and I have to see this from her point of view. Through her eyes, the pattern of events is one that proves I have been unfaithful. But I just wish she would try and see it from my point of view as well because, through my eyes, this pattern suggests one thing.

I'm being set up.

It's an extremely troubling thought, but it's the only one that makes sense, and it's the overriding conclusion I came to while I was sitting in the back of the taxi this evening on my way to check in to this hotel again. I came to the conclusion based on something Rebecca had said during our last argument, which I had brushed over at the time but is now lodged in my mind.

Having been in a tailspin and trying to come up with a plausible excuse as to why somebody else's underwear was in my wife's drawer, I had said that somebody else must have put it there. In her rage, Rebecca had snarled back that "she put them here! Right after she fucked you in our bed!" While that last part had been terribly upsetting to hear because it simply wasn't true, it was the first part of that sentence that has stuck with me.

"She put them here!"

It has to be her. The woman at the door. She must have got into my home and planted the underwear in Rebecca's drawer. She must have put the lipstick on the shirt too. This is all happening because of her, and it all started on the night she came to our house and knocked on our front door. That's the only explanation I can think of. But my wife isn't buying it. In her mind, the only explanation is that I have been caught in a lie and that I have betrayed her. Worryingly, that means it is unlikely that I'm going to be allowed back home to be with my wife again unless I can change her mind about things. But there's only one way to do that.

As the elevator doors slide open to deposit me onto the fourth floor, I take out my mobile phone with my free hand and go searching for the text message from the private investigator. I find the message as I carry my overnight bag towards the door for room 414, and I call the number for the PI as soon as I'm inside the room and the door has closed behind me.

I drop my bag onto the bed, the same bed that I had hoped I'd seen the back of when I had left to go home earlier, before walking over to the window and hoping that I get a good enough phone reception in this position because hotels are notoriously bad for giving poor phone signal. Thankfully, I can hear the call connecting, and I'm relieved that I'm not going to have to go back downstairs and stand outside to try and get a good line to hold this conversation on.

'Hello, Sam.'

The PI's welcome is a simple one, but this conversation is about to get a lot more complex.

'Erica. Thanks for picking up. I need your help.'

'What is it?'

'My wife's just kicked me out again. She found a pair of women's underwear in her drawer at home, but I have no idea how they got there. The only thing I can think of is that the woman who came to the door broke into my home and planted them there sometime this week.'

'Okay, slow down,' Erica advises me, but that's easier said than done in my current state.

'She's doing all of this! I don't know why but it has to be her! She's trying to ruin my marriage!'

'I understand, but I need you to keep calm and be patient. I'm looking into her, but it's going to take a little time.'

'I don't have time! My wife is going to divorce me!' I cry, and just uttering the dreaded 'D' word sends a shiver down my spine.

Is this who I am going to be, one of those men who society shuns because they cheated on their partner and ends up living out of a suitcase in a hotel whilst all their family and friends rally around the innocent party in the marriage? People will gossip about me and shake their heads in disgust, wondering how I could do such a thing to such a beautiful person like Rebecca. They will stop inviting me to things, either because they disagree with what I did or because their partners do, and they no longer wish to have anything to do with me. I won't just lose my wife, I could lose my whole social circle, and worse, I could lose my respect as a human being. I'd have to start from scratch and rebuild a whole new life, and who wants to do that at any age, let alone mine? Not only that but I don't want to have to start a new life. I like my life, and I love being married to Rebecca. Everything was great. Everything was perfect.

Or at least everything was until that woman came to the door.

'I'll give you a call tomorrow when I might have something,' Erica tells me. 'But in the meantime, I want you to take a few deep breaths and try and relax because trust me, if there is something going on here then we will get to the bottom of it.'

'There is something going on! That's what I'm trying to tell you!'

'Goodbye, Sam.'

Erica hangs up, probably because nobody likes being shouted at down the phone, but I worry it's also because she is unsure about the credibility of my claims. She either thinks that I'm telling the truth, in which case I am a very unlucky man. Or she will think that I have been cheating on my wife, and I'm now running through this whole elaborate scheme of hiring a private investigator just to make it look like I'm innocent. I really hope it's the former, but it could be the latter.

She could just be humouring me and looking for a way to make a thousand pounds. She might think that I'm guilty as sin and that I deserve everything that is happening to me. She might be on Rebecca's side, just like everybody else will be when my wife starts telling them all what has happened.

I slump down onto the bed beside my bag and bury my head in my hands. This is a disaster. My life is in ruins, and I haven't done anything wrong.

What's the point of that? What's the point of playing by the rules if you're going to lose anyway? I might as well have had an affair and had some fun because then at least I would have got something out of all this. Instead, I'm being treated like an adulterer when I've been nothing but faithful.

This is outrageous.

But this is now my life.

28

REBECCA

It's very rare that I phone in sick from work, but I think I can be excused for making an exception today. I called my manager at six o'clock while the sun was still down because I knew that he would already be up and on his way to the site. There aren't many construction workers who aren't morning people. Thankfully, he bought my story about me having a terrible headache and a temperature, and he told me to get myself right and only come back to work when I'm feeling up to it. I know he would have been disappointed on the inside, not least because we have several important milestones coming up this week in the project, but he can hardly tell a sick woman to drag herself into the office, can he? I feel guilty for letting him down, but then again, I've been let down too.

I've been let down by the man I trusted more than anybody else in the world.

Sam is out of the house again, but this time, he is out for good. I'm not letting him back in again, no matter how much he might beg or tell me that he is innocent and hasn't done anything wrong. I have to stay strong now and not waver in my treatment of him. He is the one who has made the mistake, so he is the one who should be punished.

So why must I be punished too?

It's easy to look at the offending party in a marriage breakdown like this and think that they are the only ones who have been punished. After all, Sam has been booted out of his house and is now forced to live out of a bag in a poxy hotel room, far removed from home comforts and familiar faces. It seems like he has lost and I have won. But there are no winners here, nor is my husband the only one to be punished. I have been punished too because now I am the one sitting in an empty house, and I will be the one who has to put on a brave face in front of family and friends when they offer me their sympathies and ask if I am okay. Of course I'm not okay, I'm far from okay, but my struggle is internal while Sam's is external. Everybody will see him moving out and starting again somewhere else, but they won't see the damage this has caused to me on the inside.

The sucker punch to my stomach. The stab in the back.

The broken heart.

With work being one less thing to worry about today, I can try and get started on tackling some of my other problems, the overriding one being what to do about the complete disaster that is my marriage. To say I felt sick to discover another woman's underwear in my bedroom would be an understatement, and that sickness hasn't left me yet, even several hours since I first found those knickers in my drawer. They are no longer in the house, although I'm not exactly sure where they are now. That's because I came out of the bathroom as Sam was leaving through the front door, and I threw them out at him as he went. I hope he picked them up off the driveway and disposed of them correctly, but he might have just left them lying there for any pedestrians to see as they stroll past my house. I imagine some people would get a good giggle at spotting ladies' underwear outside a house, while some people might be mortified.

But one thing is for sure.

Their reaction to seeing it will never top mine.

Before I go over to the window and look out to see if there is any incriminating evidence on the driveway, I decide to pick up the phone and call my parents. So far, it's only Ally who knows about my recent problems with Sam, but it's time I let some more people in on the news. I purposely hadn't told Mum and Dad about the woman at the door or the lipstick because I was still holding out hope that there was a more innocent explanation and, in that case, I wouldn't have wanted to worry them, nor judge Sam sceptically if it did turn out that he had done nothing wrong. But now there is little doubt that he has been up to no good so it's time to tell my parents about it and they can judge him all they want.

Mum and Dad always liked Sam and I know they will be shocked at what I am about to tell them he has done. Mum will probably feel that same wave of sickness in her stomach while Dad will most likely be consumed by an anger that I too have felt over these last few days. Mum will be disappointed while Dad will want revenge, but one thing that they will both have in common is that they will want what is best for me. It's that knowledge that is making me call them now because

I need the security that comes from having people who have my back unconditionally without making any judgements against me.

As the phone rings, I feel a strange sense of guilt come over me because I know that I am about to ruin my mum and dad's day. They're retired now, so they have most likely got a relaxing Monday planned, pottering around the garden or taking a drive out to the seaside for a nice walk. That's what they tend to do during the week these days, and it's nothing less than they deserve after a lifetime of hard work and providing for me as I grew up. But their pleasant existence is about to be shaken to its core by my admission that my perfect marriage is not as perfect as it once was, and now I am in desperate need of their support again. They would have thought that I was all settled in life with my husband, my home and my career and that they had done a great job in setting me up for adulthood, safe in the knowledge that I was well taken care of when they eventually came to pass away. But now I'm about to let them know that is not the case and that I'm in as much of a mess now at the age of thirty-eight as I was back when I was eighteen and coming home drunk with no idea what I was going to do with my life.

'Hello, love.'

My father's voice at the other end of the line instantly brings tears to my eyes because it's good to hear him. This is one man who I can genuinely trust to never let me down or hurt me. I used to have two men like that in my life, but now it's just dear old Dad again.

'Hi, Dad,' I say, fighting back tears.

'Is everything okay?'

'No, it's not,' I reply, and I'm already blubbing.

'What's happened?'

He sounds concerned, and that only makes me cry even more because I know how much he cares about me and how much he's going to hate seeing me like this when I go to his house soon.

'Sam's gone. I've thrown him out.'

'Why?'

'He's been seeing another woman.'

'He's been what?'

Dad sounds incredulous, as I had expected, and part of me suddenly worries that he is going to demand to know where Sam is so that he can go round there and sort him out right now.

'Is it okay if I come home?' I ask, wiping my eyes. 'Just for tonight. I need a break from here.'

'Of course it's okay. Do you want me to come and pick you up?'

I smile at how kind my father is.

'No, I'll drive round myself. I'll be there soon. Sorry if you had plans.'

'Don't be silly. Your mother and I will be here when you arrive.'

'Thanks, Dad.'

I put the phone down before the emotion really takes hold of me, and I let out several deep sobs as I sink onto the bed and hit the duvet with my fists. At this time on a Monday morning, I should have been on site at work fulfilling my duties in the role that I have worked hard to attain. I should have been bantering with my colleagues without a care in the world, content with my life and everything within it. And I should have been able to enjoy a few pleasant moments when my mind would have drifted to thoughts of Sam and how his Monday morning was going, giving me warm feelings of happiness and satisfaction that there was a person out there in the world who was also thinking the same things about me right then.

Instead, here I am, lying on my bed crying my eyes out and preparing to go back home to my parents, where I will attempt to assess the state of my life and how I can best piece it back together from here.

As Monday mornings go, this has to be the worst one ever.

29

SAM

I knew I should have phoned in sick today. The office is the last place I should be with everything that is going on in my life. I wonder if Rebecca has gone to work. I doubt it. I have tried calling her and I have left her a couple of messages, but unsurprisingly, she hasn't responded to any of them. I really hope she is okay, but it's unlikely. Her heart has been broken, completely unnecessarily, but until I am able to figure out a way of proving it then she will continue to be in pain, and I will continue to be on my own.

Except I'm not on my own. I'm sitting in a meeting room with six other people, and I have only just realised that every single one of them is currently looking in my direction.

'Sorry?' I say, suddenly sitting forward and trying my best to make it look like I haven't spent the entirety of this meeting in a daydream.

'We were just wondering if you could give us any more updates on the Morgan Report.'

That request came from Ed Burnstein, the director of the company I'm employed by and a man that nobody wants to disappoint. Unfortunately, I am going to have to disappoint him.

‘I’m actually still working on the latest figures,’ I mumble back, fumbling around with some of the papers in front of me as if they could possibly help me.

‘We were rather hoping that you would have something to present to us today,’ Ed replies, and even though I am looking down at the paperwork on the boardroom table, I can feel his glare on me as I flounder.

‘Err, yes. I know, and I’m sorry about that but-’

‘We’re just waiting on a new model to come through for us. But we should have the figures for you tomorrow, if that’s okay?’

I look up at the woman who has just tried to save my bacon and see Maria nodding her head at me as if I’m supposed to agree with the little lie she has just told.

‘Tomorrow it is then,’ Ed says, closing the file that was open in front of him. ‘9 AM in my office.’

With that, the meeting comes to an abrupt end, and everybody gets up from their seats to leave the room. I gather up my paperwork, which proved to be of no help to me whatsoever during that meeting because I hadn’t been listening to a word anybody had been saying, and head for the door, where Maria is already waiting for me. As everybody else leaves, she closes the door behind them and turns to look at me with some concern on her face.

‘Is everything okay?’

‘Yeah, fine. Why?’ I reply quickly, but probably a little too quickly for it to be convincing.

I know that I’m a terrible liar, but I’d rather try and make out like everything is fine than admit to my colleague that my marriage is falling apart and I’m currently living in disgrace in a hotel room with sticky stains on the carpet.

'You seemed distracted in the meeting. I wasn't sure what was going on with you.'

I realise then that I haven't thanked Maria for helping me out during the meeting with her intervention when the eyes of my boss and his fellow board members were on me. If she hadn't interrupted then things could have been very awkward for me indeed because Ed would most likely have realised that I hadn't been paying attention to him, nor had I done the work that I was supposed to have done before the meeting began.

'Thank you for what you just did then,' I say to Maria. 'You didn't have to try and cover for me.'

'I know I didn't, but we're teammates and we've got to look out for each other, right?'

I smile and nod my head. 'Right.'

Maria gives me that dazzling smile of hers, the one that gets the rest of the men in the office all worked up when she shows it to them, before she reaches out for the handle to open the door again.

'Can I ask you something?' I say just before she can.

'Sure.'

I take a deep breath before asking the question, mainly because I'm a little nervous about what the answer might be.

'What would you do if you thought your partner was cheating on you?'

Maria looks surprised by the question, and I'm just about to tell her to ignore me and go for the door when she answers.

'I'd get rid of them, I suppose.'

That's fair enough, and I'd kind of been expecting that answer.

'But what if they hadn't actually done anything wrong, and it just seemed like they had.'

'You mean what if they weren't cheating, but I thought they were?'

'Yeah.'

'I don't know. That's a tough one. I guess it comes down to trust then, doesn't it?'

'What do you mean?'

'Well, if all the evidence is pointing in one direction, the only way I could ignore it would be if I trusted my partner more than I trusted the evidence.'

I think about Maria's words, but I don't have to think about them for long because they seem fairly straightforward. If Rebecca has told me to leave, it means that she trusts the evidence over me. That's either because the evidence is too strong, which I'm not sure it is, or it's because her level of trust in me was not as high as it could have been to start with. My wife is looking at me like I'm the bad guy, but maybe she is to blame too because here I am, as innocent as the day we first met, yet she doesn't trust me.

What does that say about her?

'What's this about?' Maria asks me after I have failed to respond to her. 'Has something happened at home?'

‘At my home? No, of course not,’ I lie, trying to laugh to show how ridiculous an idea that is. ‘It’s just a friend. I’m trying to help him out with his wife.’

‘Oh, I see. A friend. That’s a shame. I hope everything works out okay.’

Maria gives me that smile again before opening the door and leaving the room, and while I’m not entirely sure that she believes my question was about a friend’s marriage rather than my own, I appreciate the fact that she didn’t probe any further.

I’m about to follow her out of the room when I decide to make a quick check on my phone to see if Rebecca has made any attempt to get in contact with me. I’m not going to call her again right now or send any more messages this morning, but I’m hoping that she has got back to me to at least let me know that she is okay. But there are still no notifications from her, which is not a good sign. But there is a notification from somebody else on my phone screen.

I have a missed call from the private investigator.

Closing the boardroom door, I put my phone to my ear as I call Erica back, my heart beginning to race in my chest as I wonder what it could be that she has to tell me. Has she made a breakthrough in her investigation into the mystery woman at the door? Does she have a name for me, or even better, does she know where I can find this woman right now? Or has she exhausted all avenues and come up dry, contacting me to simply say that she is not going to be able to help me track down that woman and that there is nothing more she can do?

I hold my breath as I hear Erica pick up the phone and thank me for returning her call before she gives it to me straight.

She has been doing some digging after using the footage of that woman to start her investigation.

And now she thinks she might have something.

30

THE WOMAN

It's probably clear by now that I'm a woman who likes to take charge of her life. I did it when I wanted Devon, the man of my dreams, and I did it when I realised that I had stumbled upon a potential business that could make me a fortune. But even for a control freak like me, there are some things I have to rely on other people to do. One of those things is intrinsically tied to the success of my business.

I need my clients to let me know if what I am doing is working.

That's why I am making a call to one of my current clients right now. I need to speak with her and get an update so I can assess the situation and decide if things are working already or if I am going to need to do more in order to achieve the desired result.

My client picks up on the second ring, which is very quick and either means that she is desperate to hear from me or simply already had the phone in her hand when I called.

'Hey,' she says. 'Is everything okay?'

'Hi. I was just about to ask you the same thing. Is there any news?'

‘Yeah, I think there is, actually. It seems like there’s a few problems at home. I’m not sure how serious it is yet, but things are definitely happening.’

‘That’s good,’ I say, because it is. ‘We’ll let things play out for now, and I’ll check in with you in a couple of days. But feel free to give me a call if you make any progress yourself in the meantime.’

‘Will do. Thanks, Charlotte.’

I hang up and put my mobile back into my handbag before taking another sip from the coffee cup that is on the table in front of me as I sit outside this quaint little cafe in the English countryside. Charlotte is not my real name, but it is the name that I gave to this particular client when I started working with her. If things go wrong and she ends up revealing what the pair of us have been up to then at least she has the wrong name to go off for starters. But I have no reason to think that things are going to go wrong.

From what my client has just told me, it sounds like everything is going to plan.

My client has told me that there are hints of trouble at home between the couple we are trying to break apart, and that’s exactly what I was hoping to hear after doing all the work I have done so far. As successful as my business is, there is no guarantee that any of the things I do will work. Knocking on a door and telling a husband or wife that their partner is cheating on them doesn’t mean that they are going to believe me over their spouse, nor does putting someone else’s underwear in a bedroom guarantee that they are going to kick that spouse out and start filing for divorce.

All I can do is try to make things happen.

But it's ultimately up to the couple themselves to decide the outcome of all of this.

I'm glad my client has given me a promising update because it means that I might be able to keep my feet up and let things go the way I want them to from here without much more work required on my part. If so, I will be getting paid the second half of the sum of money that my client owes me in good time. They only pay me half upfront, and the rest is dependent on how well my methods work.

But what if my initial methods hadn't worked so far? What other tricks do I have up my sleeve to bring about the destruction of a perfectly good marriage? Let's just say that there are very few lines that I am unwilling to cross and very few things that I am incapable of doing to achieve my desired outcome and get my full payment from my client.

Very few.

With the warm glow of the sun on my face as I sit outside this cafe and enjoy a quiet Monday afternoon, it's easy to think that everything is alright in the world. But it's not. Not really. I'm still grieving the loss of Devon, the man I loved and the man I had successfully taken for myself before he was tragically taken from me by a drunk driver. There isn't a day that goes by when I don't think about him and how much fun we would be having together if he was still around. I seriously doubt I would be in this line of work if he was here. Instead, I'd just have a more traditional job because I wouldn't care about silly things like money, power and control if I was in love. I'd be too busy laughing, kissing and making memories.

I wish he was here with me right now to enjoy this beautiful day and a lovely cup of coffee. But he would only have ordered a drink from this cafe if they had dark roast coffee beans because they are the healthiest type, and he was a very healthy guy. I had just figured that it was because he had to be healthy in his line of work as a personal trainer. But Devon didn't just look after himself because he had to portray a certain image to his clients. He did it because he was genuinely interested in health and fitness and doing what was best for the human body.

I guess it's the same for me. My clients probably think that I portray an image of being a cold and calculating woman because that's the type of work that I am in. I am a professional homewrecker, after all. But that's not why I behave this way. I am cold and calculating, not because it's my job to be, but because it's the woman I have to be now in order to survive. If I let my emotions get the better of me, I would break down in tears every day at the loss of Devon and the state of my life without him. That's why I keep all emotion out of it. I have shut myself off from the world, and nothing can get in now.

I have no regrets. I have no conscience. I have no rules.

There is no limit to what I will do these days, simply because I have nothing to lose.

I've already lost the only person I care about in the world.

So why would I care if somebody else loses that person too?

31

REBECCA

In normal circumstances, I enjoy being back home with Mum and Dad. It's a chance to relax in familiar surroundings, with a fully-stocked fridge and all the other comforts that one associates with the place where they grew up. But these are not normal circumstances, and I'm not enjoying being here. Neither are my parents enjoying having me home. That's because instead of doing what they usually do when I visit, which is keeping me well-fed and watered, they are trying to get me to stop crying and explain to them exactly what has gone wrong in my seemingly happy marriage.

I've been doing my best to give them the full run-down of events, from the woman at the door to the discovery in my underwear drawer, but I've been too upset to make much sense, and I realise that my parents are still a little unclear as to how and why I came to learn that my husband had been unfaithful. I need to start making more sense, but I also need to let my emotions out before I do, rather than keeping them bottled up because if I can't be myself here then where can I be?

My mother has her arm around me and is telling me that everything is going to be okay, even though she can't possibly know that, while my father has gone into the other room to find me a box of tissues. He had brought me one a moment ago, but one is not going to be enough, so he has scurried away for reinforcements. I wipe my red eyes with my hand as I wait for him to return while Mum continues to tell me that everything is okay, just like she did when I was a child when I would burst into tears after falling over in the playground. But this situation is far worse than any of those innocent times because this isn't about a scratched knee or a sore arm. I'm not crying because of a bruised bone or a bruised ego. I'm crying because somebody has broken the most important commitment to me that they could ever break.

The man who chose to forgo all other women in favour of me has broken that word and left me looking like a fool.

As Dad returns with more tissues, I thank him and take a handful before holding them over my face and weeping some more. If I was to look up, I'm sure that I would see my parents exchanging a troubled glance. But I don't look up. I just keep my face in the tissues because it's easier for me that way.

After a few more minutes of letting my emotions run free, as well as several more useless platitudes from Mum about how I'm going to be fine, I get a grip of myself and stop the pity party. A couple of deep breaths later and I am finally ready to stop being treated like a child and start talking like an adult.

I tell Mum and Dad everything. The surprise visitor at the front door. The shocking thing that she said. Sam's theory about it being some kind of prank. How I had taken his word over hers. How I had then discovered lipstick on his shirt collar. The drunken argument. Sam's move into a hotel. The reconciliation. The feeling that the worst was over. Then the moment I saw that underwear in my drawer, which has led to Sam going back to that hotel again and me being here right now on this sofa blubbing away.

The only thing that I leave out is the near-miss I had on site last Monday. They don't need to know that their daughter almost died because she was worried about her husband's potential lies.

They are going to hate Sam enough as it is without me throwing that into the mix too.

By the time I am done speaking, Mum is no longer telling me that everything is going to be okay. How could she if she had listened to what I had just said? There is nothing okay about all of that, and not even a mum with the best will in the world could pretend that there is.

'He still won't admit to anything?' Dad asks me after he has taken a seat in his armchair opposite the sofa where Mum and I are sitting.

'No,' I say, shaking my head. 'He still maintains he is innocent.'

'I'll see what he has to say about that when I go and speak to him.'

'Dad, no! I don't want you getting involved!'

'But I am involved! You're my daughter, and he is my son-in-law, and look what he has done to you.'

'Dad, please!'

'I've got a good mind to go to his office right now.'

'Christopher, that's not helping!'

Mum's stern voice, as well as the use of my father's full Christian name, lets both him and I know that the matriarch of the family has spoken, and her word is final.

Dad wisely decides to stop talking for a moment and let his wife come up with a plan instead.

'I can't believe Sam would do something like this,' Mum says with her arm still around me as if she is afraid to let go. 'I know he's not perfect, but I never thought he would do something like this.'

When Mum says Sam isn't perfect, she is simply referring to more innocent indiscretions of his, like how he is absolutely useless at DIY or the fact that he isn't the best timekeeper and has often turned up late for family lunches whenever he has come straight from work. But those things are forgivable. I didn't need a husband who could put up a shelf or who turned up for a meal on time every time. I just needed a husband who I could trust to never hurt me. *Ever.* But apparently, that was too much to ask for.

'I just want him to admit to it,' I say, looking down at the crumpled tissues in my hand. 'It's the fact that he is still lying to me that is the worst. It's like he has even less respect for me by still trying to get out of it.'

'I know, love. But he probably never thought he would get caught. He's in denial, I suppose.'

It's pretty clear from what Mum is saying that she believes me and has taken my side instantly, which of course she should do in her capacity as my parent, but a part of me feels a little disappointed. I think that's because I was almost hoping that she would have seen something in my version of events to offer me a glimmer of hope that it might not be as straightforward as it seems. Some way that Sam might still be innocent in all of this, perhaps. But just as I feared, the facts don't lie, and they are not pretty. Sam is guilty as sin. He didn't think that he would be caught, but he has been, and now it's clear that I have a very simple choice to make.

Stay with a man who betrayed me.

Or divorce him.

My father has not been quick to jump to Sam's defence either, instead preferring to talk about going to my husband's workplace and speaking to the adulterer face to face, which is a terrible idea, and I'm glad that Mum was able to nip it in the bud straight away. The last thing I need is everybody at Sam's workplace seeing him and my father rolling around in the car park punching the living daylights out of each other. They always got on so well, finding plenty in common, from football to politics, but it only takes something like this to bring an end to a friendship. Dad will always be on my side, just like Mum will, and Sam will now be an outcast from our family.

Unless I decide to forgive him and let him back home permanently.

But how can I do that?

I'll just have to try and move on because while it will be harder in the short term, it will surely be easier in the long term. I won't have to worry about where he is or who he might be with whenever he stays out late or works away. I won't have to find myself worrying whenever I hear him get a message on his phone that could be from some woman arranging another meet-up. And I won't have to find myself staring up at the bedroom ceiling in the middle of the night while he is fast asleep next to me, wondering if he is dreaming about somebody else other than me and secretly laughing at me for allowing him back into our house.

But I can't think about divorce and separation right now. I just need to think about something that will make me feel better in the moment, and my mother's suggestion of a cup of tea does just that. It's only a small thing, but it's the small things that I came here for.

The big things can wait for the time being.

I'm in no rush to deal with them today.

32

SAM

I'm in a rush today, and it's all because I'm on my way to meet Erica. But I'm not the only person rushing around. I'm in Central London at lunchtime, which means there are plenty of people with places to go and people to see. I grit my teeth as a burly man pushes past me as I reach the top of the escalator and walk towards the tube station entrance. I've managed to get out of the office and whizz across the city in order to meet Erica so I could find out what exactly she has been able to get on the woman I tasked her with looking into. To say I was excited when I heard her tell me over the phone that she had news would be an understatement because if the PI can help prove my innocence then she can help save my marriage.

I had asked her to give me the news over the phone, simply to save time and to give me a faster way of knowing if I could call Rebecca and tell her that I had something concrete to back up my claims, but Erica insisted that we meet to discuss her findings in person. That is why I am scurrying around London now on my way to the meeting point in front of The Shard.

I am seconds away from getting some answers.

As I leave the murky darkness of London Bridge station and step out into the bright sunshine of a clear day in the capital, I feel my phone vibrating in my trouser pocket, and I take it out to see it is a text message from Maria back at the office. She is telling me that Ed, my grumpy manager, came by my desk and asked to see me, but she covered for me and said I had gone to see a client. Better that than telling him that I was out on personal business when I was supposed to be finishing up a report that was already overdue. I send a quick message back to Maria, thanking her for covering for me once again, seeing that this is the second time after she saved me in the meeting this morning. Then I put my phone away and focus on the task at hand, which is not an easy one.

I have to try and spot Erica on this busy street.

Looking around through a sea of commuters and tourists, I struggle to catch a glimpse of my PI and wonder why she picked such a busy place to hold this meeting. Surely a coffee shop or a park bench would have been better than outside one of the busiest train stations in one of the busiest cities in the world.

But then I see her. She is standing about twenty yards away from me in a black blouse with a handbag over her shoulder. To the untrained eye, she looks like an ordinary woman on her lunch break. But I know who she really is.

She is a woman of means.

Or at least I hope she is.

Rushing over towards her whilst almost being run down by a cyclist going way too fast down the road, I eventually reach her and get the greetings over quickly so I can move on to the important stuff.

'What do you have?' I ask her, and Erica wastes no time going into her handbag and taking out a brown envelope.

Feeling like I'm in some kind of espionage movie, I take the envelope from her and open it up. That's where I see two photographs of the woman I have been looking for.

The woman at the door.

'You found her?' I ask, studying the two images carefully to make sure that it really is her. But it definitely looks like the woman in Steve's CCTV footage.

'Yeah, I found her,' Erica replies casually as if it was easy work, which it may very well have been. But I don't care if she didn't have to work very hard for the money I am paying her. I just care that she did her job and found this woman. But I'm not quite ready to hand over £1000 yet. I still need to know more.

'Who is she?' I ask,

'Her name is Alexandra Burton. She is thirty six years old, and she lives in Clapham in South London.'

It feels good to finally have a name to put to the face that has tormented me for so long. Now my thoughts of frustration and revenge can be spliced with more personal details rather than just an image of a blonde woman walking away from my house. These photographs show Alexandra sitting outside a cafe enjoying the sunshine.

Enjoying her life while mine falls apart.

'Okay, so why is she doing this?' I ask as I put the photos back into the envelope.

'That's what I am still looking into,' Erica replies as the lunchtime hordes of London rush by all around us.

'How did you find her?'

'I was able to get access to further CCTV footage near your home based on the direction in which she had been walking. From that, I was able to see her getting into a vehicle on a street around the corner from yours. A search on the registration plate of that vehicle gave me her name, date of birth and address.'

I'm impressed by Erica's work, although it is precisely the kind of work that I am paying her to do.

'That's great, thanks. This is a good start.'

'Yes, it is. I will continue to watch Alexandra and see what I can learn from her movements but finding out exactly what she is doing and why will require much deeper investigative work.'

I already know from the way Erica said those words that she means it is going to cost me more money if I want her to carry out that "deeper investigative work."

'How much?' I ask, cutting to the chase because we are standing in the middle of a city that was built on that mindset.

'I'll need another thousand pounds. That's for bugs.'

'Bugs?'

'Recording devices. I can place them in her home if I can gain entry or even access her phone records.

'That sounds illegal.'

‘That’s because it is.’

Suddenly an additional thousand pounds doesn’t seem too steep. Instead, I’m more worried about the fact that we are now entering territory that could see one or both of us fall foul of the law.

‘I don’t know if I want anything like that,’ I confess, starting to sweat a little and not just because of the sun beaming down on us from overhead.

‘I appreciate that, but it might be the only way to find out what she is doing. Other than going and asking her to her face, of course.’

‘Can’t you do that?’ I suggest, perhaps a little naively.

‘I could, but why would she tell me? And all it would serve to do then would be to tip her off to the fact that someone has been looking into her. She could start being more cautious or disappear completely, and then you would never know what she was really up to.’

I nod my head because Erica has a point. She is obviously good at her job and has been doing this long enough to know all the outcomes of all the different moves she could make. That’s comforting, but it’s offset somewhat by the fact that she isn’t as clean-cut of a PI as I thought she was.

No wonder her website was so basic.

She probably has just as much to hide as the people she investigates.

‘Do I have to decide now?’ I ask, wiping a bead of sweat from my forehead and glancing around nervously at some of the people rushing past us as if they can tell that this conversation might not be a legitimate one.

'No, like I said. I will keep an eye on her and see what I can find out that way. I appreciate that you don't want to go down the more extreme route, and I would prefer not to do that either. I was just letting you know that it may be the only way.'

I nod at Erica and try to give her a smile, although it feels like more of a grimace. Then she tells me that I can keep the photographs because she has copies already before she turns and walks away, only needing a few seconds before she disappears from view on the crowded street.

After watching her go, I look down at the envelope in my hand and think about the woman in these photos inside. I think about what she has done to me, and I think about what she has done to Rebecca. That's when I realise that I have to know the full story, no matter how I go about learning it. I will give Erica permission to do whatever she needs to do, no matter how risky. That's because the things she finds out could not only be the key to saving my marriage, but they could be the difference between me having peace of mind again in my lifetime or not.

I'll never be able to rest until I know why this woman came to my house and told a lie.

I'll do anything to find out.

Even if it means risking prison.

33

REBECCA

It did me good to go to my family home and spend time with my parents for a couple of days, but now I need to start trying to get a little more normalcy back into my life. That means going back to work after a few days of sick leave. It means going back to my own house after a few days of sleeping elsewhere. And it also means replying to the messages and missed calls I have from my husband after a few days of blanking him completely.

I wonder if he came by our house at all while I was away, either hoping to speak to me or just to get a few more of his things from his wardrobe. He does still have his key, so he may well have done, and if he did then I'm sure he would have noticed that the bed hadn't been slept in. It wouldn't have taken him long to assume that I had gone back to my parents, but if he did figure it out, I'm just glad he didn't turn up there and try to speak to me. That would have been a bad move on his part for many reasons, not least of which because my father would have likely gone berserk at him and told him to get lost unless he wanted a good punch in the face. Thankfully, that didn't happen, and my father didn't have to throw any punches, nor did my husband have to receive any.

It's not that my dad is a violent man, but he is fiercely protective of me, as any parent would be of their daughter, so he isn't too happy about the fact that Sam has gone and broken my heart. My mother isn't best pleased either, and even though she doesn't express her emotions in quite the same way as her husband does, I could tell that she was deeply hurt and deeply angry at what Sam has been doing behind my back. But of course, my parents are an easy audience for me. I'm always going to find sympathy there no matter what the situation. But that's not the case out in the big, bad world. There's little sympathy out there in the cold light of day, and that is where I must go now. I can't hide away at Mummy and Daddy's forever.

I have to go back to my own life.

I have to face the music.

Putting my key into the front door, I turn the lock and step inside, noticing the pile of letters on the doormat as I do. There is a couple of days' worth of post in the hallway, as is to be expected when a homeowner goes away for a couple of days, so I pick it all up and carry it into the kitchen, where I take a seat at the table and start to sort through it.

The first thing requiring my attention is an electricity bill, and it's a reminder of how even the most mundane parts of life carry on in the most difficult of times. It's also a reminder of a job Sam didn't do even though I had asked him to do it several times, which was to request that we get our bills electronically now instead of through the letterbox. Normally, I would be irritated that he hadn't listened to me, but on a scale of what he has done to me recently, this indiscretion is minor.

The second and third letters are just leaflets from local politicians canvassing for my vote in the upcoming local election, so I scrunch them up and toss them into the bin, not because I have no time for politics on a good day, but just because I have no time for it right now. Then I get to the last letter, and I tear the envelope open without even looking at the front of it, expecting it to be just more of the same kind of thing. Something boring. Something normal. Something for the bin.

But it's not.

It's actually something very important.

It is a handwritten letter, though there is no name at the bottom of it to tell me who it is from. The message is a fairly short one which means I am able to read the entirety of it quickly, but I have to go back and re-read it a few more times before I can even start to understand what it might mean.

Hello Rebecca. I am writing to you because I feel bad about what I did the other night. I was just so angry that I had to do something to get back at Sam, and that was the only thing I could think of. But you didn't deserve to find out that way. Maybe I should have just written a letter and told you like that instead of standing on your doorstep and blurting it out. I imagine it must have come as quite a shock to you. I hope you are okay. Please understand that it was never my intention to hurt you. I was just trying to get back at your husband after he hurt me.

Sam and I slept together just over a month ago like I said last week. I know it was wrong, of both him and me, but it happened. Even though I hate him now, I cared deeply for him after that and thought there was the chance of something more between us. He had certainly led me to believe that there would be. But in the end, he decided to stop communicating with me, as if he could just forget about what had happened and go back to his life without a second thought for me.

But that wasn't fair.

It wasn't fair on me, and it wasn't fair on you.

You didn't deserve what we did behind your back, but you did deserve to find out about it, so you have all the facts and know exactly what kind of man you are married to.

I hope you are okay but understand that things might not be easy for you now. Again, I am sorry about this, though I don't expect to ever earn your forgiveness. I just wish you all the best, whatever you decide to do.

I turn the piece of paper over to check that there isn't any more writing on the back, but it's blank. This is all there is, although there's more than enough here to wrap my head around. It's a letter from the woman who my husband cheated on me with.

It's a letter from the woman who came to the door.

She has clarified her comments that night, as well as expressed remorse at her actions, both that evening and the evening over a month ago when she slept with a married man. While any apology from this woman is not worth the paper it's written on, I do still find it intriguing that she has decided to make contact with me this way. As much as I hate her and despise what she did, the fact that she seems sorry suggests that she isn't the biggest villain in all of this.

That would be Sam, the man who has screwed us both, literally and figuratively.

I put the letter down and decide that I need a drink before I read it again. Going into the fridge, I'm relieved to find that there is one more can of vodka and tonic at the back, and I take it out and open it up. Then I retake my seat and study the letter again as I drink, my eyes scanning the words that were composed by the hand of the woman who tempted my husband to break my heart. I remember her being attractive from the night I saw her at my front door, but it's clear from the way she has written this letter that she is also smart too. It is very well put together and structured, even though I hate every word of it, and I wonder which quality it was exactly that proved irresistible to my husband in the end.

Her brains or her beauty?

It was probably a combination of the two, just like Sam said it was a combination of those two attributes that had caused him to want to see me again after our first date.

To him, I had beauty and brains, and he liked that.

He obviously liked it about this other woman too.

Damn him and his weakness for the opposite sex. I wish this woman had been boring and plain so he would never have been interested in her. But I also wish that I had been boring and plain that day on the tube too because then Sam might never have given up his seat for me and started talking to me, and he would never have ended up being the man who I fell in love with and walked down the aisle for.

But it's too late for that now.

What's done is done. This letter is proof of that.

I decide to treat it like the politicians' leaflets and screw it up before tossing it into the bin to join them. I don't need to read that letter again.

Nor do I ever need to see the man who is mentioned in it either.

34

SAM

I'm emboldened by the fact that my private investigator has been able to track down the woman who has ruined my life. I'm also feeling sick about the fact that I could soon be giving the word to my PI to undertake illegal activities. It's been quite the day, and the envelope sitting on my desk is just one more crazy part of it.

I lean forward and pick it up, taking out the photos inside and looking again at the images of Alexandra. Everything about the pictures irritates me. The way she is holding her cup of coffee. The way she is sitting bathed in glorious sunlight. And the fact that I had to pay somebody a thousand pounds just to take these damn pictures.

The next time I see Alexandra, I hope I get more pleasure from it. A photo of her being hauled into the back of a police car would be nice, but there's a long way to go until Erica and I can prove any wrongdoing on this woman's part. I'll see what the PI can dig up by more legal means before I go ahead and give her the word to sneak into Alexandra's home and start planting things. But it's the thought that Alexandra must have snuck into my home and planted things of her own which means I am willing to fight fire with fire if I have to.

I'm just about to put the photos back into the envelope when I hear a knock on my office door and Maria walks in.

'Hey. Not interrupting anything, am I?'

'No, it's fine,' I say, shoving the photos back into the envelope and putting it back on my desk before attempting to cover it up with various papers.

Maria smiles and takes a seat in the chair opposite me before letting out a deep sigh.

'God, what a day.'

She's not wrong there, but I imagine she means it for entirely different reasons than I do.

'Has Ed been round again?' I ask, assuming she is ready for a good moan about our boss.

'Yeah. Once, twice. Six times,' Maria replies, and I laugh.

'Thanks for what you did again earlier for me when I had to go out. You don't have to keep covering for me.'

'I know I don't, but I want to. You'd do the same for me.'

Maria gives me a wink, and I guess she is right. I would cover for her too, because that's what teammates should do.

'Cheers,' I say before glancing at the time in the corner of my computer screen. It's six o'clock, so I should probably call it a day, but I'm not in any rush to go back to that empty hotel room and sit and think about my life.

'Is everything okay?' Maria suddenly asks me, snapping me out of my depressing daydream.

‘Yeah, fine,’ I lie. ‘Why do you ask?’

‘I’ve worked with you long enough now to know when something is wrong. So what is it?’

I think about lying and saying it’s work pressure, or something with my health or just anything that means I don’t have to tell the truth and say Rebecca has left me, but I’m a terrible liar. I always have been, and I kind of hope that I always will be because surely that has to count for something, right? But I really don’t want to let anyone else in on what is going on in my personal life because this is between my wife and I, so in the end, I decide to tell a lie, no matter how rubbish it might be.

‘I’m waiting on some test results from the doctors,’ I say. ‘I’m sure it’s fine, but it’s hard to concentrate on anything else while I wait.’

The reason I am a bad liar is because I hate doing it and especially about something as serious as health, but I had to say something to get Maria to stop probing, and health is usually a good call. People tend to respect matters like that and leave it for the doctor to deal with. But I appreciate that saying things like that can cause worry and now Maria looks very concerned.

‘I’m so sorry. I had no idea,’ she says, looking like she really means it.

‘It’s fine,’ I say, batting the air dismissively.

‘You should tell HR. Maybe they could get Ed to go easy on you for a few weeks.’

‘I don’t really want anybody knowing. It’s personal, you know?’

‘I understand.’

Maria and I sit in silence for a moment, and I feel terrible for whatever sadness she is feeling right now. For all I know, she could be imagining me dying from some terrible disease after what I have just told her, which is not a nice thing to put somebody through. But I had to think fast and I'd rather this than have everybody around the office know that I'm living in a hotel because my wife found another woman's pair of knickers in our bedroom.

'How about a drink?'

Maria's sudden invitation is an appealing one as well as a little surprising because we've never been out for drinks before as just the two of us. I tend not to go drinking that much with work colleagues, but if I have done then it has always been as part of a larger group. I would like a stiff drink right now, and a busy bar would sure beat that lonely hotel room. But I better not. I can't be going out for a drink with another woman while I'm trying to figure out a way of getting my wife to trust me, even if it is just Maria, my long-standing colleague.

'Thanks, but I better get some work done. Ed still wants that report tomorrow,' I say, making an excuse even though I'm sure I could just get it done for my boss first thing in the morning before he gets in.

But once again, Maria surprises me.

'Don't worry about that. I've already done it,' she says with a smile.

'You have?'

'Yeah, I had a couple of hours free this afternoon, so I jumped on it, and it's all done. Sorry, I should have sent you an email.'

'No, that's great! Thank you!'

I'm genuinely impressed at my colleague's help, and it does feel nice that I at least get treated well here.

If only I had this kind of treatment at home.

'So, you've got no excuse now, have you?' Maria tells me, and I guess she is right.

'Okay, one drink,' I say. 'But I'm buying. You've already done more than enough for me for one day.'

'I'm not going to argue with that.'

I laugh as I get up from my chair and grab my jacket before pulling it on and logging off my computer. I definitely feel like I could use a good drink and a laugh, and this might be just the thing I need to take my mind off my troubles for at least an hour or so. Those troubles will still be waiting for me in the morning, as evidenced by the photos of Alexandra still sitting in the envelope buried underneath the papers on my desk, but for now, I'm going to try and switch off from the world, just like I'm switching off my desktop monitor after another day of work is at an end.

As I follow Maria out of the door, I have a moment of worry that somebody else in the office might see us leaving together and make some kind of false assumption about what the pair of us might be up to outside of work. But then I dismiss the thought and tell myself that I don't care even if a colleague does see us heading for the exit together. That's because, just like the situation with the woman at the door, I am innocent. I am sick of feeling bad for things I haven't done wrong, and I am doing nothing wrong now, so I have nothing to feel bad about. This is just a drink with a colleague, a colleague who has helped me out enormously today. That's all it is.

In the end, my brief worry that somebody from work might see us leaving the office was wasted anyway because there was nobody else around. Everyone has already gone home, so Maria and I left without being seen.

Or at least I thought we had.

It turns out that I had been seen, though.

And I had been seen by the worst possible person.

35

REBECCA

I'd gone to Sam's office because I wanted to show him the letter that I had perhaps prematurely thrown into the bin after I had first read it. I had taken it out and put on my coat before boarding a train and heading into London with the intention of confronting him with it at his place of work. I could have done it elsewhere, but I wasn't patient enough to wait, and I knew exactly where he would be, so I went ahead and reached his office. I had then spoken to the man on the reception and asked if Sam was in, which had been confirmed, before being seconds away from asking if I could see him. But then I had paused, suddenly aware that this might not be the best thing to do in my situation.

As much as I was feeling angry and betrayed at the contents of the letter, which had only backed up my fears after all the other things had happened, there had still been some part of me that had realised that an argument with my husband in his workplace might not have been the fairest thing to do to him. Just because his personal life was falling apart around him, it didn't mean that his professional life had to take a hit too. Even though he was in the wrong and I was in the right, I still cared about him enough to give him the respect of not embarrassing him in front of his colleagues. That was why I had left the reception and gone back outside, deciding that I was going to wait until he was finished with his duties before speaking to him about the letter.

I had gone and bought myself a coffee from the stall on the corner before taking a seat on a bench opposite Sam's office and keeping my eyes on the door to make sure I didn't miss him when he came out. It had been late afternoon then, so I knew it wouldn't have been too long until he finished, and I was happy enough to wait because it was either this or go back to my empty house and think about how I would probably have to sell it now because it held too many memories of the man who had let me down.

It had also been pleasant to sit in the sunshine that had been peeking through the gaps in the tall buildings in this busy part of London, and I had almost enjoyed my time on that bench, even if I knew that darker times were ahead when Sam came out of that door and I told him about the letter. But time had gone by, as it has a nasty habit of doing, and the sun had slipped away behind the tall buildings leaving me sitting in the shade and feeling much colder than I had been feeling earlier. I had seen several people leaving the office as they finished their shifts, but none of them were my husband, and I wondered if he was going to be working late, meaning I would need to text him to let him know that I was here instead of ambushing him when he came out. It had been as I had taken out my phone to make contact with him when I had seen him finally leaving the office.

But he hadn't been on his own.

I had watched from my seat on the bench as my husband had walked away with another woman, laughing and joking as they went. As much as I had been hating my husband for what had happened recently, the fact that he had always protested his innocence had made me wonder if he was struggling when I wasn't around and finding it hard to come to terms with his marriage being on the rocks. But I guess that was silly of me to think like that because Sam was clearly not struggling.

He looked perfectly fine to me, and why wouldn't he be? He was walking away with a very attractive woman, and as I came to find out, he wasn't just walking with her to the train station.

He walked with her all the way into a bar.

I had wanted to go into that same bar behind them and see for myself just how much of a good time they were having in there, but I decided against it because I simply didn't have the energy for a potential argument. That's because I felt winded, as if someone had punched me in the stomach and I was struggling to get my breath while they stood over me and laughed. That was how it felt when I saw Sam walking away from his office with a big grin on his face while his pretty colleague smiled beside him.

How could he go for a drink with another woman when his marriage was falling apart?

How could he go out and have fun when he knew that I was falling apart too?

There is only one way I can see that is possible, and it is that he can do it because he is the kind of man who is able to put his own selfish desires ahead of thoughts for anybody else. Seeing him with his colleague looking like he didn't have a care in the world has made me realise that he really doesn't have a care in the world. He doesn't care that he cheated on me, nor does he care that I found out about it. For him, it looks like life goes on, and I have to wonder now how many times he has been going for drinks with this woman in the past when I thought that he was just working late. Where else have they gone together? Have they ever gone back to a hotel? Have they ever gone back to her place?

And have they ever gone back to ours?

As I stood outside that bar glaring at the entrance knowing that my husband was inside there enjoying a drink with another woman, I thought about how it could have easily been this person who came to my doorstep and told me that Sam had cheated. Why not? I feel like Sam could have been seeing all sorts of women behind my back. He sure looks like he is a hit with the ladies. It makes me mad that he protested so angrily when I accused him of cheating, but it was clearly just a defence mechanism because he had been caught out. What a guy he turned out to be.

And what an idiot I turned out to be.

I decided to walk away from that bar and not go inside to see if he was even closer with that woman than their walk into it had suggested because there had simply been no point. I'm done. I'm done with him, and I'm done with this marriage. Forget what he has done with that bloody woman who came to our door and wrote me a letter, although that is bad enough. The thing that has hurt me the most is actually seeing him smiling as he left the office because here I am dying on the inside. Who knows, but maybe if I had seen him looking all glum and moody then it might have at least given me a sign that he was missing me and couldn't go on without me. But no. Not Sammy boy. He's perfectly fine, and now he's probably getting perfectly drunk with that perfectly good-looking woman he is out with tonight.

I'm back home now, the letter is back in the bin, and I'm thinking about going back to my parents. But then I decide to do something else. I head upstairs into the bedroom, the one I spent so many years sleeping in beside the man I loved, and I take out a couple of suitcases. Then I open up the wardrobe doors and all the drawers in here and start taking out Sam's stuff.

His shirts. His trousers. His shoes. His socks. His gym gear.

Everything of his that I can find is going into these suitcases.

By the time I am finished, the room is looking a little bare, although not too bare because I always did have more clothes than him, so there's still plenty of things hanging in the wardrobe and filling up the drawers. But at least his stuff is no longer clogging up my space.

After zipping up the suitcases, I carry them out of the bedroom and down the stairs, feeling the strain in both my arms, but my determination overpowers my muscle fatigue, and I make it to the front door. Unlocking it, I step outside and dump the suitcases on the driveway, ready for Sam to pick them up when I tell him where they are. Then I go back inside and close the door, leaning against it and breathing heavily.

As I get my breath back after my excursion down the stairs with the luggage, I feel better for what I've just done. I've begun the process of moving on. At least superficially, anyway. But the real moving on won't happen unless I make my separation from my husband official.

That means getting a divorce.

And that means everybody knowing about it.

36

SAM

I'm glad I went for a drink with Maria. It helped to take my mind off things for a short while, and it felt good to have a reminder that not every woman in the world hates me at the moment. Alexandra hates me, although I still don't know why. Rebecca hates me because of what Alexandra has done. And I'm sure that Rebecca's mum hates me after I have upset her daughter.

But at least Maria doesn't hate me. She's a good colleague and a good friend, and she is also a good drinker. She had plenty of wine while we were in the bar after work, and that is why I can excuse what she did at the end of the night when it came time to say goodbye.

She made a pass at me.

Of all the shocking things that have happened to me recently, my colleague moving in to give me a kiss is perhaps the winner. I had no idea that Maria even liked me in that way. To be fair to her, she had apologised immediately and told me that she had made a mistake before saying that she knew I was married and she had simply had too much wine that night. While I had been stunned at the unpredictable turn of events, I had told her that it was okay and that I didn't think any less of her for what she had done. She seemed relieved about that but no less embarrassed, and she had made a hasty exit then, hailing a taxi and fleeing the scene as if I was the police and she was a criminal with a bag full of stolen money.

I have thought about messaging Maria and telling her to forget about it for the fear that she might be up all night worrying about seeing me in the office in the morning, but I've decided to leave it. As drunk as she is, I'm just as drunk too, so messaging anybody in my current state is not a good idea. Instead, I'm just going to lie down on my hotel bed and try and get some sleep so I'm not too hungover when I hand that report to Ed tomorrow.

As I sink into the lumpy mattress that contains none of the comfy contours that my bed at home has, I turn my thoughts away from Maria and think of my wife instead. God, I miss her. I just want to see her and ask her how her day was. I just want to make her laugh and witness that smile of hers when I tell her about my day. And I just want to have her head on my chest as we fall asleep together, me stroking her hair while she whispers something about the future and all the exciting things that we have ahead of us.

But that's not happening. I'm here all alone, and she is elsewhere. Maybe at home or maybe with her parents. Wherever she is, I just hope she is missing me too. But I doubt it.

I expected that I would fall asleep quickly after consuming so many beers tonight, but that isn't the case, and I'm still awake thirty minutes after lying down and closing my eyes. That's annoying because these days, sleep is the only way I get to switch off. Being awake means thinking about my troubles, and I've had enough of thinking about them.

Getting up off the bed, I go into the tiny bathroom that comes with this hotel room and pour myself a glass of water from the tap. Chugging it down my parched throat, I pour myself another before returning to the bed and slumping down onto the edge of it.

Looking up, I catch a glimpse of my reflection in the mirror on the wall opposite me, and I look as bad as I feel.

Dishevelled. Drunk.

Dire.

It's easy to see why my wife might be better off without me when I look like this, although it's also difficult to see why Maria was so interested in making a move on me this evening. I haven't shaved for days, nor have I slept much, so I was hardly looking my best when she decided to go in for a kiss. But that's the danger of drinking too much, I suppose.

Alcohol can turn anybody into an oil painting.

As I sit there looking pale and pathetic, I wonder how Maria is feeling. Maybe I should message her, after all. I hope she isn't awake, fretting over things. I did genuinely mean it when I told her that it was okay and that she should just forget about what she did. But that might be easier said than done. We do have to work together for forty hours a week, and I'm not sure how plausible it is for either of us to completely forget what happened.

I am surprised that she did make a move, even though she was drunk. She knows all about Rebecca because I've told her about my wife plenty of times. She must have gotten a glimpse of the wedding ring on my finger every day when I was handing her papers and taking them back in return. And she has definitely seen the photo of Rebecca that I used to keep in my office to look at until Ed took over the company and told all staff to remove personal items from the office because it looked unprofessional.

With all that considered, it is strange that Maria would think that she could try and kiss me and that I might reciprocate. She must have known that I was going to say no, yet she tried it anyway. Maybe she is lonely herself, which is something I had never thought of as being a problem for her. Someone who looks that good surely doesn't have any trouble finding a man, and I know there are plenty of men in the office who would happily trade in their wives to be with her, but appearances can be deceptive, I guess. She might be just as lonely as anybody else.

She might be just as lonely as me.

I'm glad that I didn't tell Maria about my problems with Rebecca, although she could surely detect that something is not quite right with me. I'm not sure if she bought my lie about my worries over some 'test results,' and I'm almost certain that she saw through my poor attempt at pretending it was "a friend" who was having problems dealing with false accusations of cheating, figuring out that it was me I was talking about instead. But she didn't probe, and I'm glad about that.

She just tried to kiss me instead.

A shiver runs through me as I think about how awkward it is going to be for the pair of us at work tomorrow. I need a way of breaking the ice quickly, making a joke and letting her know that everything is okay, and we can just carry on being the great teammates that we are. That should be simple enough, and it's about time I had a simple task.

I've got more than my fair share of difficult ones still ahead of me.

As well as dealing with Maria and my hangover tomorrow, I am going to have to contact the private investigator again and tell her to do whatever she has to do to get me some answers. I can't waste any more time on this. I can't spend another night in this damn hotel. I'm also going to go back to my house after work and have another go at speaking with Rebecca. It might be a disaster, but I have to keep trying because that will hopefully show that I haven't done anything wrong and that I won't give up on us no matter what.

Tomorrow is shaping up to be a busy day, so I should probably have another go at trying to get some sleep. Shuffling back on the bed, I put my head on the pillow again and close my eyes, thinking about recent football results because that is one topic that won't cause me any stress and should ensure I drift off quicker this time. Sure enough, it works, and I'm fast asleep a few minutes later, my intoxicated mind dreaming of all sorts of weird and wonderful things as it tends to do whenever I have consumed alcohol this late in the evening.

But one of the dreams quickly turns into a nightmare, and it's because I see her standing in that doorway. *Alexandra.* The woman who started the nightmare when I was awake is now starting nightmares when I'm supposed to be resting.

I hate this bitch.

Why did she pick me?

Why must she torment me?

And most importantly, what do I have to do to defeat her?

37

ALEXANDRA

I've been doing this long enough now to know that it is going to take something extra special to stop me. I have a 100% success rate when it comes to breaking up the marriages of the targets my clients pay me to, and I also have a 100% success rate in getting away with it. Nobody has ever been able to prove what I have done to them, nor has anybody ever been able to correctly identify me and investigate me further. But that's not down to good luck on my part. Rather, it's down to me being clever, prepared and elusive.

I always use a fake name. I always work in areas where nobody will recognise me. I wear gloves so that I don't leave fingerprints, whether that is when breaking into a target's home or when I post the letters I sometimes like to send. Most of the people I do this to won't even suspect that something is wrong until it is far too late, by which time I am long gone, leaving nothing but their broken marriage in my wake. But even if anybody fancied their chances of finding me and figuring out who I am, I think several steps ahead to make sure that doesn't happen. I take risks like going to the door and speaking to the homeowner, but only after everything has been considered, and I'm sure that I will be able to get away easily. I've mapped out several escape routes should my first one be blocked. I've ensured that there are no home surveillance cameras installed that overlook the driveway and could capture my image approaching the front door. And I park several streets away so I can make my escape in a vehicle that nobody will see the registration of.

I love what I do, but I'm only able to keep doing it if I get away with it. That's why I'm only ever as good as my last job. Make a success of it, and I get to move on and cash in somewhere else. Make a mistake, and I'm done.

So far, no mistakes have been made.

And I'm not planning on making any in the future either.

One potential mistake I could make is by thinking ahead to the next job before the current one is complete. That is why I never look too far ahead, preferring to stay present and take each day as it comes, or rather, each target as they come. That means my mind is still very much focused on Sam and Rebecca, the couple who I am currently in the process of dismantling.

My latest update from my client sounded promising, but I decided to turn the screw a little further by writing and sending a letter addressed to Rebecca in which I clarified what I had said to her the night I went to her door. Knowing that a wife will always hate the mistress, I have found this tactic of sending an apologetic and guilt-ridden note to be highly effective because it can disarm the wife and bring her onto my side, creating an even bigger gulf between her and her 'cheating' husband. Rebecca should have received and read that letter by now, which means she should be even more determined to get Sam out of her life, thus freeing the poor man up for another woman who harbours desires for him.

Another woman like my client.

I expect we are moving into the end game now, making it just a short matter of time until I get word from my client that Sam's marriage has moved into the area known as 'irreconcilable' and that she is happy because now she has a chance to make her move on the man. Maybe she has made her move already, too impatient to wait. I wouldn't have advised that she do anything at this point, but it can be worth a shot if Sam is the type of guy who needs a shoulder to cry on and who could be tempted into forgetting about his marriage troubles by a little attention from somebody else. The worst that could happen would be Sam turning her down, but that doesn't mean something can't happen in the future. It just means he isn't ready for it yet because he is still thinking about his wife and the slim chance of recovering the marriage. But give it time, and he'll come round. They all do. That's because perhaps the most fundamental thing that underpins the total success of my business is not sex, lust, desire, greed, love, betrayal or revenge.

It's loneliness, or rather, every human being's need to avoid being lonely at all costs.

Nobody wants to be on their own, despite what they might say. Human beings thrive on social contact and affection from their fellow man or woman, which is why Sam will eventually start to crave affection from elsewhere now that he won't be getting it from his wife. He might think that it's Rebecca or nothing, but he'll soon realise that it's not as much about who the woman in his bed is but that there is a woman in there at all.

His wife. My client. He thinks he prefers one over the other but remove one and he'll gladly take the other option.

I've removed Rebecca now, which means my client can swoop in and claim the spoils.

This is a fun job, and the closer it gets to the end, the more fun it becomes.

Let the games begin.

38

REBECCA

The loud shouting from my husband in the downstairs hallway gives me the hint that Sam has come around and noticed his belongings packed into suitcases on the driveway. I knew this moment was coming, and I also knew that it wasn't going to be easy, but it's a moment that has to be passed through in order for us both to get to the other side.

'What the hell do you think you're doing?' Sam cries as I appear at the top of the stairs and look down at his flustered face.

'What does it look like I'm doing?' I reply, keeping calm so as not to mirror his extreme anger. 'I'm kicking you out.'

'By putting all my stuff on the driveway?'

'Yes.'

'What if somebody had stolen it all? You could have at least told me!'

'Maybe I should have done. You'll have to forgive me, but I was a little distracted by the fact that my husband is a cheating rat who has been up to all sorts behind my back.'

Sam looks furious, and I'm not sure if it's just about the suitcase situation or whether it's because I am calling him out on who he really is as a man. Either way, he looks so angry that the thought crosses my mind that he might start doing a lot more than shouting. He looks like he wants to punch a hole in the wall, and I worry for a second that I might have pushed him too far, even after what he has done to me. But fortunately, he doesn't put any holes in the wall, and he seems to calm down after a few tense seconds of him glaring at me from the bottom of the stairs while I look down at him from the top.

'Can you come down here? I have something to talk to you about,' Sam says before he walks away into the living room.

'I have nothing more to say to you!' I call after him, but I get no response, and it's clear he isn't going to leave until I engage with him a little more.

Reluctantly plodding down the stairs, I find him in the living room sitting on one of the two sofas, so I take my seat on the one opposite him.

'What?' I ask, with plenty of venom in my voice.

'Remember the private investigator I talked about? The one I said I was hiring to find out who that woman at the door was?'

'You know exactly who the woman at the door was! You slept with her!'

Sam looks like he wants to argue back, but he grits his teeth and calms himself down again before going on.

'My PI found her. Her name is Alexandra.'

'Fine. Make up whatever fictitious story you want to make up about her. But I know the truth. She sent me a letter.'

Sam looks as shocked as I had expected him to be about that news.

'A letter?'

'Yep. She confirmed what she had told me that night at the door, and she said she felt sorry for me and that she knew it was wrong. At least somebody is apologising for what's happened.'

'Where is this letter?' Sam asks, looking around the room, but I just wish he would stop pretending like he can get out of this by acting dumb.

'I threw it away.'

'Why?'

'Why do you think? Because it made me feel worse!'

'I could have given it to the PI to look into!'

'Stop talking about a stupid PI! Just admit you're guilty so we can get on with things!'

Sam frowns as he processes what I just said to him before he asks me another question.

'What do you mean get on with things?'

'I mean divorce, Sam. That's what I mean.'

'Don't be stupid. You can't divorce me over this.'

'Why not? You cheated on me. What do you want me to wait for? Another woman at the door?'

'Can't you see she is doing all of this? She's manipulating you into leaving me even though I've done nothing wrong!'

'Why would she do that?'

'I don't know why yet. That's what I'm hoping the investigator is going to find out. That's why you need to tell me if this woman gets in touch with you again. It could be useful!'

I'm going to scream if I have to hear about this private investigator one more time, but before I do, I decide to pull Sam up on what I saw him doing yesterday.

'Actually, I was going to show you the letter she sent yesterday. I went to your office and was planning on giving it to you when you finished.'

'You did?'

Sam suddenly looks very puzzled, and I wonder if it's because he is now wondering if I might have seen him with his female colleague. But he won't have to wonder about it for long.

'Yeah. I sat on a bench opposite your office, and I waited for you to come out so I could speak to you about that letter. But I didn't get the chance to do that. Why? Because I didn't want to interrupt all the fun you were having with that pretty colleague of yours.'

'I wasn't having fun. She was just trying to cheer me up.'

'It looked like it was working!'

'You've thrown me out! Forgive me if I needed a distraction from how bad my life is. What do you want me to do? Curl up into a ball and cry?'

'Yes! What do you think I've been doing?'

'But I haven't done anything wrong, and you just need to believe me!'

'That would make things easier for you, wouldn't it? If I just believed you. If I just pretended like a woman hadn't told me about you and her and if I hadn't just seen you walking into a bar with some office floozy while my heart was breaking into a million pieces!'

'It was just a drink! Nothing happened!'

'I'll have to take your word for that because I left before you came out. Just like I took your word all the times you told me that you loved me and that I was the only one for you.'

Sam suddenly gets up off his sofa and comes towards me and I'm not exactly sure what he is planning on doing. But then he drops to his knees and grabs my hands before looking me straight in the eye.

'You want to leave me? Fine. We can get a divorce. I'll sign whatever you want me to sign, and you can tell people whatever you want to tell them about me and what I have supposedly done. If that is going to happen then that is what will happen, and there is nothing I can do about it.'

I'm relieved that Sam has finally grasped the severity of our situation now, but there is something in the tone of his voice that makes me wait to see what he has to say next.

'But if there is one part of you, one tiny part that still thinks there might be a chance for us then you have to give me the opportunity to fight for us, and the only way I can do that is by proving that I am innocent and that woman is guilty.'

'Sam, I…'

'-Wait, I'm not done,' my husband tells me, and he keeps a firm grip on my hands with his face only a few inches away from mine as he kneels before me. 'If I have done this and I have cheated then the PI won't be able to find anything, will she? All of this will be an expensive waste of my time and you can divorce me then because I won't have any way of explaining what has happened.'

Sam nods at me as if to let me know that he is speaking sense, and I have to agree that he is.

'But let's just say for one second that I am telling the truth here. Then the investigator will get something, and that will show that I have done nothing wrong. Isn't that chance worth fighting for? If you're going to divorce me anyway then what have you got to lose? Just give me another day or two to try and find something on this woman. We already have her name. Now we just need to find out why she is targeting us.'

I can see tears in my husband's eyes, and his impassioned speech has clearly stirred up his emotions. It could all just be another act, of course, but I really hope it isn't and not just for the sake of our marriage. It's because if he is still lying to me now then he is damn good at it, and it means I know him even less than I thought I did. Telling fake stories is one thing, but shedding fake tears is another. That requires a different level of acting, and it's not a level that I care to even think about.

'Just another day or two. I'm telling the investigator to do whatever it takes, and I'm certain she will prove my innocence then. Just give me this last chance. You don't have to let me back home but hold off on the divorce until you know beyond a shadow of a doubt that I am guilty.'

I have tears in my eyes as well now, and I feel one of them running down my cheek as Sam holds onto my hands and pleads with me to give him a little time.

'Fine. A couple of days. That's it. Then I'm divorcing you.'

It sounds crazy but Sam actually seems happy with what I have just told him, and he thanks me before getting back to his feet and heading for the door. Either he's extremely deluded, or he really is innocent and is expecting to have the evidence to prove it soon.

I guess I'll find out soon enough.

Either my husband is a cheating liar, or he is the victim of some sick woman's game.

I think it's the first, but I hope to be proven wrong by it being the second. But what would that say about the state of the world if it is the second? What would it mean if there is somebody out there going around ruining people's marriages by spreading a web of lies?

It doesn't bear thinking about.

Then again, neither does divorce either.

39

SAM

After the shock of going to my house and seeing my clothes in suitcases on the driveway, I have managed to regroup and buy myself a little more time before Rebecca can forge ahead and file for divorce. But that's all it is. Just a little more time. Without some hard evidence and tangible facts to prove my innocence, there is no doubt that Rebecca and I are finished.

That is why I'm now on the phone to Erica to get another update from her.

The last time I spoke to her was this morning when I had given her full authority to do whatever she had to do to get me the truth about Alexandra. Recording devices. Cameras. Phone hacking. Whatever it took, and whatever it cost, I wanted my PI to know that nothing was off-limits anymore.

'Hi, how's it going?'

My first words to Erica sound like the words of a man greeting a friend after having not seen them for a few days. Casual. Open-ended. Carefree. But that's not what my words mean at all in this case. In this case, I want to know how things are going in terms of the illegal operation I have given Erica permission to execute on my behalf.

'Sam, I wasn't expecting to hear from you so soon.'

'I know, but things are happening here, and I'll be honest with you, Erica. I'm getting desperate. My wife is going to divorce me, and she is going to do it quickly unless I can prove my innocence.'

'How quick are we talking?'

'I've got a couple of days, max.'

There's silence at the other end of the line, so I waste no time in filling it.

'Is that going to be a problem?'

I sincerely hope not, but I have to find out if the self-imposed deadline I just gave to my wife was really a bad idea and one more nail in my coffin.

'You're really not giving me much time to do my thing,' Erica replies, but I choose to look at her response as a positive one because she hasn't shut me down completely yet.

'So what have you done?' I ask.

I hear a deep sigh at the other end of the line before I get the answer.

'I have hired an assistant who I have used in the past, and he is going to help us gain access into Alexandra's home this evening.'

I didn't realise Erica had an assistant at her disposal, and maybe it's a sign that I'm paying her too well.

'How is he going to do that?'

'He will create a distraction so that he can gain access to Alexandra's home and plant the recording devices that will hopefully give us more insight into what she is up to.'

'Okay. That's good. You say you're doing this tonight?'

'That's right.'

'You can't do it right now?'

'I'm going as fast as I can.'

'I understand.'

It's not fast enough for me, but I'll have to be patient. If bugs are being planted around Alexandra's home this evening then we may very well have some answers by the morning.

'What else are you doing?' I ask.

'My assistant is keeping watch of her while I see what I can do about accessing her phone records.'

'You think you can do that?'

'If you are asking if I have done it before then yes, I have. Can I do it for Alexandra? I don't know yet, but if I can then be sure it will be done.'

'That's good. Please, do what you can. I just want my wife back.'

Erica says nothing, and I wonder if it's because she is too professional to offer sympathy or whether it's because she feels too awkward to reply. In the end, I just tell her to call me soon and then hang up.

With that call taken care of, I pick up the two suitcases that my wife ever so kindly put outside the house for me and drop them into the back of my car before getting behind the wheel and starting the engine. As I drive back in the direction of the hotel where I will spend yet another lonely night, my thoughts are not on what might happen with Erica, her assistant and Alexandra tonight but rather the fact that my wife saw me leaving the office with Maria yesterday. I have to admit that would not have been a good look for me to have been seen going into a bar with a woman while my marriage was on the ropes. I obviously had no idea that Rebecca was going to see me doing that, but that's not the point. The point is that I should have kept refusing Maria's invitation for a drink until she got the message before going back to the hotel and having an early night. That way, Rebecca would have had one less thing to be mad at me about, and I would have looked more like a sorrowful guy rather than a guy who was in the mood for drinks with a pretty woman.

Not going for the drink would have also meant not having the awkward moment when Maria tried to kiss me, and it was that awkward moment that led to several more awkward moments in the office today. I guess it was slightly optimistic of me to think that things between the two of us could go back to normal after she made a pass at me and I turned her down. We're still both professional enough to get on with our jobs, but it was evident today that there is a tension between us now, and it's one that means things might never be the same again. This time yesterday, I thought Maria was just friendly to me because we worked together, but now I know that it is because she likes me. How can that not change the dynamic between us? With my awkwardness and her embarrassment, I'd say it's going to be a while before we are having a conversation that doesn't feel loaded with subtext and confusing thoughts.

As I drive on back to my dreary room for the night, I decide that I am going to make more of an effort to let Maria know that I want us to still be good friends. As inappropriate as what she did was, I can put myself in her shoes because I know how it feels to be lonely. I'm feeling lonely right now, and the only way to combat loneliness is to seek out the company of another human being. That is all Maria was doing yesterday. She was trying to combat her loneliness. Therefore, I can't be too hard on her, nor should she be too hard on herself.

Bringing my car to a stop at a set of traffic lights, I find myself checking my phone again as if there is going to be a message or a missed call from Erica with some new information that is going to get me out of the mess that I find myself in. But there isn't, and that is hardly a surprise considering it's been less than ten minutes since I last spoke to her. I need to give her time to work, and I need to be patient. But that's easier said than done when I'm driving around with my suitcases in the back of the car while Rebecca sits in our house and searches online for cheap divorce lawyers in the area.

Hopefully, tonight will be the night when I finally get some good news. Hopefully, tonight will be the night when I can prove my innocence to my wife.

And hopefully, tonight will be the night when Alexandra's little game is over.

40

ALEXANDRA

I sometimes get frustrated with how slow my days can be when I'm waiting for my methods to work and for my client to confirm that I have successfully broken up a marriage. But today is not one of those days. That's because the sun has been shining over South London, and I took the chance to get out and enjoy it, spending a lovely afternoon on Clapham Common with a good book and a bottle of wine. I was feeling a little tipsy when it came time to stand up and walk home but fortunately, my flat isn't far from the common, so I didn't have too much distance to cover before I made it to the comfort of my living room sofa. That is where I am parked now with my feet up on my coffee table and the TV playing a film in front of me.

It's eight in the evening, and I am winding down, just like the day is. I expect I will be in bed within the hour, an early night for sure, but I could use the sleep. It could be any day when I get the word that Rebecca and Sam's marriage is over, and that will mean I get paid before I begin this whole process all over again.

Find a new client. Lay some new traps. Break some more hearts.

And make plenty more money.

At least an early night was the plan anyway. But that idea was shattered by the fire alarm in my complex sounding, ruining the peace and causing me to get up from my comfortable position to go and look for my shoes.

'Damn it,' I mutter under my breath as I put on some suitable footwear before grabbing my jacket and heading for the door.

I know it's not a drill because the building manager would never do a drill at this time of night, but I'm hoping that it's just a mistake and there isn't really a fire somewhere in this building now. If there is then it could be a while before I am allowed back into my flat, and that would be annoying.

It's not that I have much in here that I'd be afraid to lose in a fire.

I just really want to have that early night.

Unlocking my door, I step out into the corridor and see a couple of my neighbours leaving their homes, looking just as confused and irritated about this whole thing as I am. I've never made much of an effort to be friendly with the people who live in the flats next to me, and that is perhaps why none of them say hello to me or ask me how I have been as we all head for the staircase and start descending down.

I can't see or smell any smoke, so that has to be a good sign, but I carry on going downstairs and go outside to the front of the building to join my neighbours at the designated meeting point where we are all to wait until the fire brigade get here and give us more information. I assume those fire engines are on their way towards us right now because they are supposed to get an automatic notice from the security company who manages this building whenever an alarm sounds. But it will take some time for them to arrive, and all there is to do until then is cross my arms and try and stay warm until I go back inside.

It was warm earlier when the sun was beaming down on the common, but it's chilly now that it has disappeared behind all these buildings and plunged London into darkness. I'm just glad I managed to get my jacket on before leaving the flat. I can see at least two people out here in their pyjamas.

As me and the rest of the displaced residents continue to find out whether or not their address is at risk of burning to the ground, the alarm continues to blare, and it's giving me a headache, so I could do with a distraction. I reach into my pocket for my phone, but it isn't there and I realise I must have left it in my flat in the rush to leave. That's annoying but it's hardly as if my phone was going to give me much entertainment anyway. I'd like to say that I would have several unread messages waiting for me from all my family and friends to show how popular I am, but there will be nothing as usual. That's my own fault because I've purposefully withdrawn myself from all the people who I used to know in my former life, which is how I refer to the time when I wasn't going around the country ruining people's relationships. Moving to Clapham was a big step for me because I'm originally from the North of England and knew nobody in London, which was precisely why I chose it. It has helped me out professionally because I don't have to worry about telling anyone I know what I actually do for a job, but it's not been much good for me when it comes to receiving messages. The only messages I receive these days are from clients giving me updates and while that's good for business, it's not great for my social life.

I'm all alone down here, or at least I am if you don't count the people standing near me in their pyjamas. That means there isn't much to occupy me, and I'm almost fearing that I might have to strike up an inane conversation with one of my neighbours just to speed time up a little when I hear the fire engine coming towards us.

I appreciate that some women get a kick out of seeing a man in uniform and especially one wielding such a phallic symbol as a hosepipe, but I've never been one of those women. To me, a fireman is just that. A fireman. A guy doing a job. Nothing sexual about it.

They certainly don't have a patch on Devon, my hunky personal trainer who would be keeping me warm if he was here with me now.

I'm better off not thinking about the man I lost, so I just watch the firefighters going into the building to make their checks, and it's a good sign that they aren't taking their hosepipes inside with them. I like to think that means that there is no fire and this is all just one misunderstanding, and sure enough, that much is confirmed twenty minutes later. A bald chap who looks far too chubby to be a fireman takes off his helmet and tells us all that we are okay to go back inside. There is a stampede for the entrance doors as one might expect, and I join the hordes heading back into the warmth, trudging my way up the staircase before reaching the door to my flat and going inside.

It's a relief to close the door and hear the silence that comes from the alarm no longer being activated. It's also a relief to go into my bedroom and start getting ready for bed. Unlike some of my neighbours, I'm not in my pyjamas already, but it doesn't take me long to change that, and it's only seconds later when I'm under the duvet preparing to turn out the light. But just before I do, I notice something wrong in my bedroom. It's only a minor thing, but I know when something is out of place. That is why I get out of bed again and go over to investigate.

Reaching the wardrobe door, I look closely at it and see that it is open slightly, just as I suspected. That's no big deal if I had left it open myself, but I know that I didn't. I always ensure that the wardrobe is closed completely, and when it is, the edge of the door is flush with the rest of the unit. But the door now is ajar slightly, and that's how I know that somebody has been in here. That would be disconcerting at the best of times for somebody who lives by themselves, but it's made even worse by the fact that I keep important things in my wardrobe.

That's why I always ensure the wardrobe is closed.

It's because I know what could be found if somebody other than me was to open it.

Opening the wardrobe door fully, I frantically go inside it and start moving the strategically placed boxes that I keep on the top shelf. As I do, I silently curse myself for never getting a better security system for some of my paperwork than this makeshift system that I came up with. I should have got a safe or at least some kind of locked box, but I didn't. I just naively assumed that these things would be safe as long as they were out of view because why would anybody ever break in here anyway?

The items I am looking for now are a series of documents that relate to my clients. I get each of them to sign an agreement before I go into business with them, and while there's nothing particularly incriminating itself in the wording of the documents, it's the names within them that could be used against me. The names of every single client I have ever had are on these papers, and while they might not mean much by themselves, together they could be used to piece together my sordid business if somebody knew the significance of what they were looking at.

That's why I am frantically looking for the documents now.

And that's why I am extremely relieved when I find them.

Taking out the wedge of papers from beneath one of the empty shoeboxes that they were buried beneath, I quickly count them to make sure that not a single document is missing. I've had thirty-one clients in my time, so there should be exactly thirty-one pieces of paper here. Thankfully, that is the number I reach after counting them, so that at least means that nothing is missing. But that still doesn't explain why my wardrobe door was open.

The door I am always so careful to keep closed.

I wonder if a firefighter might have accessed my flat during their checks to make sure that the building was secure, but I find that unlikely because surely they would have had to tell me if they had entered my home. But if it wasn't them then who? One thing is for sure. Somebody has been in here. But why? And how did they get in? The front door was not damaged in any way. The more I think about it, the more I am convinced it has to be the firefighters. They were looking for all potential sources of fire. They were just being thorough. The owner of the building must have given them a key, and that was how they accessed my home.

That makes sense, or at least it makes me feel better than the alternative does. It's the alternative that somebody came in here because they know who I am and what I am up to, and they are looking for evidence to bring me down. But I'm just being paranoid. Nobody knows who I am, and nobody knows about my business other than the people who hire me to carry it out.

I'm safe.

Nothing is missing, and that means that nothing is wrong.

So why do I feel so sick?

41

REBECCA

It's been a busy day, and not just because it was my first official day back at work after my time off with sick leave. I took the leave because I needed some time to deal with the shock of my marriage collapse, and I'm glad I did, but I couldn't put off going back forever. Alongside being on site, sitting in meetings with grumpy foremen and dodging excavators as they moved over the mud, I have also been busy making plans for my friend's hen party, which is scheduled to take place four months from now. Her name is Rachel, and she is an old friend from my school days and Ally and I are her joint maids of honour. That means not only do we get to be with her as she prepares to walk down the aisle on her big day, but we also get to arrange the event that will signal an end of her 'single' days and send her headlong into matrimony.

You might think that helping plan a hen party for an upcoming marriage might be difficult when my own marriage is falling apart around me, and you would be right. But it's not Rachel's fault that my husband turned out to be a liar and a cheat, and that's why she deserves to have me give it my best shot when it comes to helping plan her hen party. I haven't even told her that I am having trouble with Sam, and I will leave it a while before I do because she has enough going on in her life right now with all the wedding planning without me drawing on her time with sob stories about women at the door and letters through the post. But I am planning on getting plenty of things off my chest tonight, and Ally is the perfect person to help me do that.

I walk through the wine bar and see my best friend sitting at one of the tables texting on her phone, so I walk over behind her and call out her name, making her jump because she hadn't noticed me coming.

'You're such an idiot,' she tells me as she puts her phone down and gives me a hug, and I laugh before I take my seat and scoop up the wine menu.

'Are you ready for a fun night of hen party planning?' Ally asks me as she puts her phone into her handbag and zips it up, letting me know that I have her full attention for the next few hours, not that I would expect anything less.

'I am, actually. This is just what I need to take my mind off things.'

'Things still bad with Sam?'

'I'd say we've left bad behind and progressed onto doomed.'

I let out a sarcastic chuckle to try and keep things light, but Ally doesn't buy it, and she takes my hand to get me to stop looking at the menu and look at her instead.

'Oh, Becca, what's happened now?'

'Remember that woman who came to the door? The one who said she slept with Sam. Well, she wrote me a letter too in which she said that she felt guilty about what she had done but that it was still all true.'

Ally winces, and I bite my lip because I can feel the emotion threatening to overwhelm me again. Fortunately, a handsome waiter arrives at our table at that perfect moment and gives me the distraction that I need to keep the tears at bay and instead focus on the very important task of deciding what bottle we are going to select from the menu.

My friend and I make a quick decision on what we want to drink for the next hour or so, and the waiter scurries away to fetch it for us so that we can go back to lamenting my poor choice of husband.

'What has Sam said about all of this?' Ally wants to know. 'Is he still denying it?'

'Yep. He's still maintaining his innocence. But I just can't trust him anymore. It makes no sense for a woman to visit me and write to me if she wasn't telling the truth. It would be the weirdest thing ever, right?'

Ally ponders it for a second before reluctantly agreeing.

'So what are you going to do?' she asks me as I watch the waiter standing by the bar in the distance with an empty tray that will soon be holding our drinks.

'We're finished. I know that much,' I reply, shaking my head. 'I just need to pull myself together enough to start making it official.'

'I'm so sorry.'

'Yeah, me too.'

The mood at the table has dropped drastically over the last few seconds, and I am aware that is my doing, so I should probably try and change that. But it's easier said than done when all I can think about is my husband and his philandering ways.

'I went to Sam's office last week to show him the letter I got in the post,' I say, watching the waiter carefully put the wine glasses onto his tray before he makes the journey back over to us. 'But guess what I saw? I saw him leaving with some woman from his office, and they went into a bar together. He was laughing away as if he didn't have a care in the world.'

'What? Who was she?'

'She's called Maria,' I reply. 'I didn't know that at the time, but I was having a look around on Sam's company website yesterday, and I found her photo. Maria Garcia. Very exotic, hey?'

I know it was slightly stalkerish of me to go looking for Maria online so I could put a name to her face, but the sight of the two of them walking together and laughing together had been eating away at me. It makes it easier to dislike someone if you know their name.

'Do you think he's seeing this Maria?'

'I don't know. Maybe. Maybe not.'

'You didn't hang around and see where they went after?'

'No, I just wanted to go home.'

'Fair enough. But you're right. That is not the way you want your husband to behave if he's supposed to be convincing you that he didn't cheat.'

I nod my head while feeling pleased that the waiter is now walking towards us, his tray balanced in his hands and a look of concentration etched across his poor face. I'm positively parched by the time he reaches us, and my first sip of wine is a refreshing one.

'But I don't want to be a downer tonight so let's not talk about me and my problems anymore,' I say as I put my glass back down on the table. 'Tell me all about you and Phil. Are you guys still going strong?'

Ally laughs, and it's good to hear that sound because this night was in danger of becoming very depressing if I just talked about Sam for the duration of it. I'd much rather hear about my friend's thriving love life than talk about my own dying one, and then after that, we can get to the small matter of the hen do planning.

As weekday nights go, this is shaping up to be a good one.

Who knows, maybe I can do this kind of thing more often when I'm single again. Girls' nights could replace the old romantic Saturday nights with Sam on the sofa. That's not what I wanted, but it seems it's what is going to happen now. That's because, as stupid as it may seem, I did give Sam a couple of days to prove his innocence to me. It's stupid because he is waiting for some private investigator to do something for him, and it's stupidity that makes me not want to tell Ally the full story. She must think that I'm gullible enough for falling for a man as deceptive as Sam without me telling her that I am waiting to see if some PI can pull off a miracle and prove my cheating husband right. But that two day deadline ends tomorrow and, so far, he has failed to come back with anything.

Of course he has failed. A guilty man can't prove his innocence. Only an innocent man can do that.

And that is one thing my husband is not.

42

SAM

It's weird being in the office so late at night. I've never worked beyond seven o'clock in the evening before, but now it's almost nine and I'm still here. But it's not as if I have suddenly discovered the elixir of hard work or anything like that. I'm still here at this time of night because I'm afraid to leave. That's because leaving means going back to the hotel room. And the hotel room is a glimpse of the grim future that awaits me.

I was hoping to be presenting my wife with some form of evidence tomorrow that would prove to her that I haven't cheated on her and that the woman at the door was lying. I had hoped to make that happen by getting a call from my private investigator with some news that would prove Alexandra's guilt and my innocence. Was that too much to ask? I guess so because the clock continues to count down to tomorrow and I still have nothing.

Sliding a fifty pence piece into the vending machine in the staff room, I select the option that will deliver me a can of cola and watch as a mechanical arm picks it up from its tray and drops it down into the bottom where I can scoop it out. Cracking it open, I take several thirsty gulps of the fizzy liquid before wiping my mouth and heading back in the direction of my office, which is on the other side of the open-plan space where so many desks now sit empty and idle, their owners having long since logged off and gone home to where their partners are waiting to welcome them in with open arms. I'm sure they wouldn't be quite so keen to leave work if they had nothing but a takeaway on a hotel room bed to look forward to, but it seems that it's just me with that problem in this company tonight, so here I am all alone.

Walking back into my office, I close the door and slump down in my chair before guzzling the contents of the can and tossing it into the bin that sits in the corner about ten yards away. Just like everything else in my life recently, it seems I'm out of luck because the can hits the rim of the bin and bounces back out instead of going in, leaving the can to roll harmlessly away across the carpet to give the cleaner another reason to detest me when she arrives in the early hours of the morning.

Letting out a deep sigh, I stretch my arms out above my head before tapping on my keyboard to let my computer know that I am still here and willing to work in case it decides to activate the screensaver again and I have to log in, which would be annoying. If my computer could talk then I have a feeling that this one would tell me that I look pathetic and that I should call it a night and quit while I'm behind. But my computer cannot talk, so that voice comes to me only as internal dialogue, which is actually worse in a way.

As I sit there typing up an email that I should have sent yesterday, my eyes feel heavy, and it seems that my tiredness is negating the effects of the caffeine from the cola can I just consumed. But a loud bang in the open-plan office outside my door gets my attention, and I stand up from my seat to see what might have caused it. I am definitely the only person here, so it's a little worrying that I just heard a noise like that, but then I realise I am wrong.

I was the only person here.

But not anymore.

Maria is walking across the office, her coat on and her laptop bag slung over her shoulder, looking like she is ready for another day of work. But the only problem with that is the working day is over. So why does she look like she is just starting?

Walking out from behind my desk, I open my office door and look out, and that's when it's Maria's turn to almost jump out of her skin at a loud noise that she wasn't expecting.

'Sam! You almost frightened me to death!'

I would normally apologise for that, but the sight of her terrified face coupled with her panicked Spanish accent is actually quite funny, and I can't help but laugh. Of course, I feel bad instantly and try to stifle it, but that only makes it worse, and now I've got the giggles. It must be the adrenaline running through my system after I heard the loud noise, or maybe it's the caffeine from the cola kicking in, but now I am really laughing hard, and it's not long until Maria has joined me.

By the time we both pull ourselves together, I have invited her into my office, where I have decided that it's time to do something that I swore I would never do.

Drink alcohol in the workplace.

As Maria tells me about how she came back to the office to pick up a report that she had left behind, I open the bottom drawer of my pedestal and take out the bottle of whiskey that I won in the Christmas raffle last year. I've never been a big whiskey drinker, which explains why the bottle has sat in my drawer unopened for months, but there is something about tonight that makes me feel like saying what the hell. Tomorrow promises to be a terrible day when my PI tells me that they have nothing on Alexandra and I realise I have not just blown a load of money on my silly pursuit of the truth but also blown any chance I had of getting Rebecca back in my life.

With that in mind, I might as well get blind drunk and add a hangover to tomorrow's proceedings as well.

'Fancy a drink in the kitchen?' I offer Maria as I crack open the bottle and gesture towards the door.

'I don't know if that's a good idea,' she tells me, and I smile.

'It's definitely not a good idea, but you know me. When have I ever had a good idea in this place?'

Maria laughs and follows me out of the room, telling me that she will stay for one, which is all I need because at least I will have some company for the first of what will most likely be far too many drinks this evening.

I manage to procure a couple of cups from the kitchen cupboards while Maria takes a seat at the table where so many of our colleagues have their meals at a more respectable time than this. Then I pour two hearty measures of whiskey before slotting another fifty pence piece into the vending machine and getting another can of cola out of it so that we have something to help the spirit go down more smoothly.

'Cheers,' I say as I raise my drink, and Maria says the same thing as she bumps her cup against mine.

We both take a thirsty gulp, and it's only then that I notice I have taken out our manager's cup. Ed will not be happy if he found out that two of his employees were sitting in the office kitchen drinking whiskey, but he would be even more annoyed if he found out that one of them had been doing it while using his beloved Ipswich Town mug.

'See, I told you things didn't have to be weird between us after what happened the other night,' I say to my colleague with a wry grin, and she bursts out laughing, which is the exact reaction that I was hoping to get from her.

'Yeah, not weird at all,' she replies sarcastically with a roll of her eyes, and I smile before taking another sip of my drink which is far too strong and will definitely be giving me a pounding headache in the morning if I have more than one.

'Why do you like me?' I suddenly ask, and the question is out of my mouth before I even have a chance to analyse it internally.

'Sorry?' Maria asks, clearly confused as to why I would ask her such a direct thing.

'The other night when you tried to kiss me. I was just wondering why me? Why not any of the other guys who work here?'

Maria thinks about her answer for a second before giving me a deadpan answer.

'How do you know I didn't try and kiss all the other guys in the office first, and you were the last one left?' she replies, and it's a good answer.

I laugh and shrug my shoulders, admitting that she might have a point before she corrects me and gets serious for a moment.

'I don't know. I guess I've always liked you. Ever since we met here. It was in this room, actually. I was being shown around the office on my first day, and you were in here using the vending machine. Do you remember?'

I do remember it. I remember it well, and the reason for that is because of how Maria looked when I first saw her that day. She certainly didn't look like any of the women I had ever worked with before. But I think it might not be wise to say that, so I just nod my head and let her continue.

'You were polite to me, just like all the other guys around here were. But you were different in that you were obviously not just doing it because you found me attractive. You were doing it because you were nice. I could tell that from the second I met you.'

'So that's it? I'm a nice guy?'

‘Well, that was how it started. Then I saw how hard you worked at your job. I saw how kind you were with me when I was still learning how things worked around here. And I saw how beautiful your wife was in the photo in your office, and I guess the fact you were taken made me start to think about you even more.’

I’m aware that what started out as a light-hearted suggestion for a drink in the kitchen is now quickly descending into something much heavier, and I know I should nip it in the bud before it gets any further. But I don’t, and there’s a good reason for that. It’s because it’s been a while since somebody told me how nice I was. I’ve had nothing but my wife telling me how bad she thinks I am recently, so it’s fun to hear someone tell me that I’m not so bad. It’s particularly fun coming from a woman who looks like Maria.

Is the whiskey affecting me already?

It must be because now I’m not thinking about how bad Rebecca has made me feel anymore.

I’m thinking about how good Maria is making me feel instead.

‘I’m sorry I tried to kiss you the other night,’ Maria says to me, sitting forward in her seat and looking me in the eye.

‘I told you not to worry about that,’ I reply, but Maria shakes her head as if I have misunderstood what she means.

‘No, I mean I am sorry for trying because trying isn’t good enough,’ she says, her eyes looking down at my mouth now. ‘I should have kept trying until you kissed me back.’

With that, Maria moves forward and brings her lips towards mine and this time I don't pull away. Our lips are only inches away from connecting when I feel the vibration in my pocket from my mobile phone, and it's just enough to snap me out of my trance and drag me back to reality.

I was just about to kiss a woman who is not my wife.

What the hell am I doing?

Getting up from my seat, I apologise to Maria before waving my phone at her and telling her that I have a call to take. She looks annoyed but stays where she is sitting as I leave the kitchen and look down at my mobile to see who is calling me.

I'd have a hard time not feeling guilty if it was my wife.

But it's not.

It's my private investigator.

'Erica!' I say into my phone, my elevated voice reflecting how shocked I am to find out that she is calling me. 'Have you got something? Please tell me that you have got something?'

There is a pause at the other end of the line before she replies.

'I have got something.'

'You have? That's great! What is it?'

'Alexandra is a woman who gets paid to break up happy marriages,' Erica replies calmly, but calm is not a word that can be used to describe my reaction to that news.

'She's what?'

'People hire her to break couples up. It seems she does it by spreading lies and planting false evidence. You and Rebecca were obviously one of her targets.'

'What? Why?'

'It would seem that there is somebody who wants to be with you, which means they needed to get rid of Rebecca first.'

'Who the hell would do that?'

'I have a name that I believe you will recognise,' Erica replies, and I slump down into an empty office chair before she has time to say it. But I'm not expecting any more shocks now. That's because I feel like I'm already looking at the woman whose name I am about to hear.

I keep my eyes on Maria sitting in the staff kitchen as I wait for Erica to tell me that it is my colleague who has been doing all of this to me and my wife so that she could stand a better chance of starting a relationship with me. It all makes sense. She has tried to kiss me. She told me that she had liked me since day one. She liked me even though she saw the photo of my wife.

But it's not Maria's name that comes out of Erica's mouth a second later.

It's Ally.

43

ALLY

I've spent the last two hours sitting with Rebecca listening to her talking about Sam, but that's nothing compared to the years I have spent listening to her tell me all about the man who I wish was with me instead of her. Rebecca tried to change the subject a few times tonight, including when she asked me about my current boyfriend, Phil, but I was always able to steer the conversation back onto the only things that I care about.

Her, her husband and the current state of their marriage.

'Stop me if I'm being too personal but have you thought about what is going to happen with the house?' I ask Rebecca before taking another sip of my wine.

'I haven't really thought that far ahead,' she admits, and I nod my head in understanding but decide to add a few words of advice too.

'Of course, I understand,' I say. 'But when the time comes and if you do want to stay, make sure you put the reason for divorce as adultery on Sam's part rather than just saying it's irreconcilable differences. That way, you have more chance of getting things you want when it comes to dividing things up with the lawyers.'

It sounds like pragmatic advice, sensible if a touch insensitive, but I'm not just doing it because I want to see my friend stay in her nice house. I am doing it because I am pushing the boundaries and seeing how serious Rebecca really is about divorcing her husband.

It's not just me who needs to know. So too does the woman I have paid to get Rebecca and Sam into this perilous position right here. Her name is Charlotte, or at least that is the name she gave me when we first met after I found her on an online forum suggesting that she could help anybody get the man or woman of their dreams, no matter their current relationship status. To say I was sceptical would have been an understatement, but with little to lose at that point, I had made contact. I say I had little to lose because I've spent years watching my best friend date, marry and frolic with a guy who I love too.

I know Rebecca says that she fell for Sam the first time she met him on the London Underground, but I fell for him the first time that I met him as well. Unfortunately for me, that first time was when Rebecca was introducing me to him as she brought him to a friend's party.

It was clear that my best friend was smitten with this new guy, and I couldn't blame her. He was gorgeous, funny, smart, with a good job, great fashion sense and a wicked sense of humour. He was exactly the kind of man I was looking for. But my best friend had found him first.

I tried to tell myself that it was just some silly crush on my part and that it would ease off when I started dating my own men and looking for my version of 'Sam.' But it didn't happen. As I went from one dating disaster to another, I watched on as Rebecca became more serious with Sam until he eventually popped the question to her and put a ring on her finger.

It was on their wedding day that I realised I didn't just have some kind of crush on Sam. I actually loved him. Not only that, but I was actively envious of my best friend and how happy she was to have snared a guy like him. As I sat there in the church in my bridesmaid's dress, watching Rebecca and Sam tie the knot, I had clenched my teeth and done my best not to cry. The tears had got the better of me in the end, but luckily, nobody knew they were tears of pain rather than joy. That's the thing about weddings. You can get away with crying because everybody thinks that you are just happy for the bride and groom.

Nobody suspects that it is because you are secretly in love with the groom.

I had hoped that the finality of seeing the man I loved get married to my best friend would snap me out of my silly state of mind and force me to draw a line under my feelings so that I could move on and focus on my own future happiness. But that didn't happen. If anything, my feelings for Sam only became stronger the more I listened to Rebecca tell me about their honeymoon or when I visited their new home for their housewarming party. I lost count of how many nights I cried myself to sleep alone in my poxy flat while I knew that they were both snuggled up together in their king-size bed. It got to the point where I had almost stopped eating because I felt physically sick. I even had to pretend to Rebecca that I had picked up some virus from a work trip abroad when she noticed my weight loss and showed concern.

I was lying to Rebecca when I said I couldn't see her sometimes simply because I couldn't face another day of her telling me all about Sam. I was lying to my employers when I told them that I was sick and needed a day off simply because I'd been up all night crying. And I was lying to all my friends and family when they teased me and asked why I wasn't settling down yet with a man of my own, simply because the man I wanted was already taken.

I felt like I was lying all the time.

But worst of all, I was lying to myself.

Then I found the woman who told me she could get me what I wanted. She could do the impossible. She could break up Rebecca and Sam's marriage, giving me the chance to swoop in and claim him for myself.

I paid the first half of the money, and I told the woman to get to work, and get to work she did. Now Rebecca and Sam are separating, meaning he will be a single man again. That doesn't guarantee that I will be able to get with him, I'm aware of that, but it does give me a chance, and that is all I can ask for. With Rebecca out of the way, he will surely be more open to the idea of the two of us being together when I do eventually make my move in the coming weeks.

Sam will be shocked to find out that I like him because I've done a very good job of keeping my feelings disguised. But his level of shock will be nothing compared to Rebecca's. She will feel betrayed when she finds out that I have made a move on Sam after her, and she will hate me if I enter into a relationship with her ex-husband. It will be the end of our friendship, that is for sure, but that is a sacrifice I am willing to make to be with the man of my dreams.

Time will tell if my plan has worked, but it seems to be working well so far. The only area of concern at the moment came when Rebecca told me about some woman called Maria Garcia who was spotted entering a bar with Sam one night after work. The last thing I need after getting rid of one love rival is the emergence of another one, but I'm sure I can handle her too.

If I can get rid of Rebecca, I can get rid of anyone.

Speaking of Rebecca, my best friend has been getting progressively more inebriated as our evening has gone on, and that is made evident by how she continues to open up to me even more about her personal problems.

'I just can't get the thought of him and that woman out of my head. Do you know what I mean?' she asks me, and I nod my head.

I know exactly what she means because I spent years with the thought of Rebecca and Sam in my head.

'I wasn't going to tell you this but fuck it. Why not?' Rebecca says, finishing off the rest of her wine and slamming her empty glass down on the table. 'My husband is so deluded in thinking that he can get out of this that he has hired a private investigator to look into the woman who came to our door.'

Rebecca scoffs and waits for me to laugh or at least show my disapproval. But I don't do that.

I'm too busy panicking.

'He's done what?'

'He's hired a PI. God knows what they are supposed to find out, but it's all a waste of time. Sam can pretend he doesn't know that woman all he wants, but his game is up.'

I try to keep calm as I process this information, but there is no doubt that it is concerning. Rebecca might think that her husband is just stalling or trying to get off the hook, but I know different. I know that Sam is innocent, and now I know that he has hired a private investigator to prove it.

I need to warn Charlotte. I need to tell her to be careful.

But what if it's already too late?

'I'm really sorry, but I'm going to have to go to the little girl's room,' I say. 'This wine is going right through me. I'll be right back!'

I get up from my seat and scurry away from the table, taking my handbag with me because I need to use the phone inside it.

I take out my mobile as soon as I'm out of Rebecca's sight and find the number for the woman who I have been paying to break up my best friend's marriage. Then I dial it, pressing the phone to my ear and trying to keep my breathing under control so I can impart the crucial information that I have just become savvy to.

But there is no answer. Damn it. I'll have to send a text.

My fingers fly across my phone screen as I type out a warning to Charlotte.

Sam has hired a private investigator to look into you. Be careful!

Then I'm just about to press send before adding one more sentence.

This can not come back to me!

I send the message and wonder what kind of response it will get when it is read. Of course, at that time, I expect it to only be Charlotte who reads it.

I had no idea that the private investigator was going to read it too and pass it on to Sam.

By then, it's only a matter of time until Rebecca reads it too.

44

REBECCA

I'm feeling the effects of the wine now and should probably slow down, but it's not every night that I get to unload all my problems onto somebody else. Poor Ally. She came out tonight for some fun, yet I've spent most of the evening talking about Sam and what he has been putting me through recently. It's no wonder she has been a while in the toilets.

She's probably dreading coming back to the table and being subjected to more of my moaning.

As I wait for my best friend to return, I reach into my handbag and take out my phone, wondering if Sam has made any more attempts to plead his innocence to me since I have been here this evening. If so, I am expecting a message or two, or maybe even a missed call.

What I'm not expecting is to see my screen full of notifications.

Twenty missed calls from Sam and twelve text messages.

What the hell?

I'm just about to open the first of the messages when Ally returns to the table, swaying slightly and looking a little flush in the face.

'I'm really sorry, but I think I might have to call it a night,' she tells me as she holds onto the back of her chair for support. 'I didn't realise how drunk I was until I stood up.'

'That's okay. I think I've probably had more than enough too,' I reply, and I put my phone back into my handbag, figuring I'll just look at all the messages when I'm in the taxi home.

Based on the sheer volume of notifications from Sam this evening, I can only assume that he has been drinking heavily in some bar of his own and has lost the filter that tells him when to stop bothering me and go to sleep.

Getting up from my chair, I put on my jacket and follow Ally to the bar where we both pay our half of the drinks before stumbling outside into the chilly evening air.

'I'm sorry to bail out early, but we'll catch up again very soon, okay?' Ally tells me, and I smile because she is still worried about me even in her state.

'That's fine. Maybe we can go for another walk this weekend?'

'Sounds good,' Ally replies as she takes out her phone to presumably try and book a taxi.

I do the same, but before I open the app that will find me a driver in the local area, my curiosity gets the better of me, and I go into the multitude of messages that Sam has sent me.

'I think Sam's been drinking tonight,' I say as I open the message stream. 'He's been blowing up my phone with messages and calls.'

'He has?'

'Yeah, I'm not sure what he wants but…'

My voice trails off when I read the first message. He tells me that the private investigator has evidence. But it's the second message that really gets my attention.

It tells me that Ally is behind it all.

'Is everything okay?' Ally asks me as she stands beside me, waiting for her taxi to arrive.

But I don't answer her. Instead, I keep on scrolling down through the messages, becoming more concerned and confused as I do.

'Rebecca?'

That's when Ally touches my arm, and I'm so on edge that it causes me to jump, sending my phone flying from my hand down onto the pavement below.

My mobile clatters across the concrete, but that's the least of my worries as I turn and look at the woman standing beside me.

'It was you?' I ask her as I look into her eyes.

'What?'

'You sent that woman to my house? You tried to break up my marriage?'

Ally holds onto her look of confusion for a few more seconds.

'Rebecca, I'm not sure what you think has happened but-'

'The private investigator has the evidence,' I reply, and that shuts Ally up just as a car pulls up to the kerb in front of us.

I'm guessing it's the taxi she booked because I didn't get a chance to book mine. I was too busy reading all the messages from Sam about how Ally's name had been discovered in that woman's apartment.

'I have to go,' Ally tells me as she makes a move towards the taxi, but she's not getting away from me that easily.

Grabbing her by the hair, I pull her back towards me and demand that she tells me the truth. The poor taxi driver looks terrified and quickly drives away, but if he's afraid then it's nothing compared to how worried Ally should be as I wrestle her to the pavement.

If it wasn't for the security guard coming out of the wine bar and pulling me off my former best friend then there's no saying what I might have done to her. But I do get pulled off Ally, and that's how she manages to run away from me before I can get any answers out of her.

I let the security guard know that I'm not going to cause any more trouble before picking up my phone from where it lies on the pavement and checking the device for damage. There is a huge crack running across the screen, but it's still usable, so I'm able to call my husband and hear his voice.

I'm crying. I'm out of breath. I'm not making any sense.

But Sam doesn't care.

He just tells me that he wants me to come home.

45

SAM

When I hired a private investigator to prove my innocence to my wife, I had envisioned all sorts of scenarios. But not a single one of them consisted of me finding out that my wife's best friend was the person behind all of this.

I thought that Alexandra was the biggest villain.

But it turned out to be Ally instead.

I'm standing outside my house waiting for my wife to get back home so that I can present her with all of the evidence that I have on her best friend and the woman who came to our door. The evidence is substantial, and my private investigator was worth every penny in the end. Erica has saved my marriage, and I will be eternally grateful to her for that. But something even bigger might come out of all this. It might not just be my marriage that is saved.

It might be dozens of other marriages too.

It's clear that my pursuit of the truth has uncovered a much bigger scandal than I could have ever anticipated. That's because I'm not the first person that Alexandra has played this game with before. She has done it to numerous couples all over the country, and I dread to think how many divorces and broken hearts can be attributed to her and her despicable business. But time will tell because my investigator and her assistant are currently combing through all the evidence and piecing together the full story of just how much of a homewrecker Alexandra has really been.

The lid was blown off this whole sorry affair when the PI's assistant was able to gain access to Alexandra's flat by setting off a fire alarm and causing an evacuation of the building. With Alexandra and all her neighbours outside, the assistant had snuck into the flat using a key that had been cut specifically to fit the lock of the target's home. It was in the flat where they were able to discover paperwork in a wardrobe that would lead to the unravelling of the business Alexandra had clearly worked so hard to build for herself.

The assistant had sent images of the paperwork to Erica, who had begun the process of trying to figure out what it all referred to. It wasn't immediately clear in the wording of the documents, but there were two names on each piece of paper, and they seemed to refer to couples.

Mine and Rebecca's names were on one of those pieces of paper.

It was through Erica's use of the internet that she was able to figure out what all these couples might have in common. By scouring social media, the PI was able to ascertain that every single one of these pair of names had been in a relationship before.

But not anymore.

That was when Erica had realised that Alexandra had not just come to my house and told a lie. She had gone to several houses and told several lies. But while there was a clear pattern indicating a troubling connection, it still didn't explain why Alexandra had targeted my marriage. Fortunately, Erica's assistant had one more trick up his sleeve.

The original plan had been to plant a series of recording devices around Alexandra's flat in the hope that they would pick up her voice during private conversations, and that might lead to figuring out exactly what she was up to. But a better opportunity had presented itself when the assistant had entered the flat because that was when he noticed Alexandra had left her mobile phone behind when the alarm had gone off.

Using technology that is far beyond my realm of understanding, the assistant was able to gain access to Alexandra's messages and contacts as well as being able to install a bug on the device that allowed all future communications to be monitored. That was how Erica was not only able to figure out who had employed Alexandra to ruin my marriage but also see the message this evening in which that person had tried to send a warning about an investigation into her.

It was Ally.

I had messaged and called my wife several times during the evening ever since I was told that Ally was the person who was really trying to break us up. But Rebecca hadn't responded to any of my urgent communications. At the time, I had thought it was because she was mad at me. But in reality, it was because she was too busy enjoying a night out with the woman I was trying to warn her about.

Thankfully, Rebecca eventually read my messages and found out about the kind of best friend that Ally really was. My wife has just called me and told me that she is on her way home in a taxi but not before she apparently confronted Ally and demanded the truth. The thought of my wife getting into a catfight on the street outside a wine bar is a troubling one, but I'm just glad she is okay. Apparently, Ally got away, but she will get her comeuppance soon enough. Erica's assistant is keeping an eye on her home now while Erica herself is keeping watch on Alexandra.

I need to make a decision on what happens next, but I don't want to do that alone.

I will do it with my wife.

Rebecca should be home any minute, so I keep watch on the road at the front of our house for any signs of her taxi. I had gone inside when I first got here, but that was when I was looking for my wife before I knew that she was out this evening. Since finding out where she is, I have been waiting outside the house because I still want Rebecca to feel like it is her decision to let me back inside for good. The evidence is now available for me to show her that I didn't cheat, but I'm aware that she is going to need some time to wrap her head around all of this. I've known from the start that this was all lies, but Rebecca hasn't, so she will need a while to come to terms with it. When she does, she will see that she hasn't lost her husband at all.

But she has lost her best friend.

I can't believe Ally wanted to break us up. I'm still not clear on why she would do that, but regardless of her motive, it's despicable. She was supposed to be someone Rebecca could trust, yet all this time she was working behind her back to ruin her marriage. To think that Rebecca and I sat across the table from Ally and her boyfriend not so long ago when all of this drama started unfolding. To think that she sat there as me and my wife got drunk and said things in public that we should have kept in private. And to think that she was taking pleasure in our pain as our marriage crumbled right in front of her eyes.

As bad as this whole episode has been for me, I'm aware it's going to have been worse for Rebecca even though it is now coming to an end. She will have to live with the knowledge that her best friend was lying to her and stabbing her in the back. I will have to make sure I am on hand to help my wife get over this betrayal, and I will do my best to help her move on.

Perhaps I could be forgiven for being resentful towards my wife for not believing me from the start, but I'm not going to hold it against her. Rebecca had every right to react in the way she did at the recent events because who is anyone to say how a person should react when confronted with the shocking claim that their partner is cheating on them? The important thing is that the truth has come out in the end, and as I see a vehicle turning onto the street, I get the sense that the end is coming now.

As the taxi comes to a stop outside my house, I rush towards it, and I am there to greet my wife as she climbs out of the back seat. She's unsteady on her feet, which could be down to the wine she has consumed tonight, or perhaps it's all the shock and adrenaline of what my investigator has uncovered wreaking havoc on her body. Whatever it is, I am there to take her in a big hug and let her know that things are going to be okay now.

She is home. I am home. We are back together again. That is all we need.

But of course, life isn't as simple as that is it. People don't just need things to go back to normal after they have been betrayed.

They need revenge.

46

ALEXANDRA

My winning streak is over. My luck has run out. My business is collapsing.

And now it's time to get the hell out of here.

If I thought the wardrobe door being open was a sign that someone had been in my flat then the text message from my client had confirmed it. In the message, Ally had told me that a private investigator was looking into me and that I should be careful. While I appreciated the warning, it seems it has come far too late. I gathered as much when Ally phoned me a short while after sending that message, and I heard her panicked voice as she told me how she had been exposed and that our targets knew everything about what we had been up to.

I tried to ask Ally exactly what she knew and how much we had been compromised, but I couldn't get much sense out of her because she was hysterical, so I just hung up, leaving her to have her meltdown in peace. Besides, it's not really worth getting hung up on the details. All that matters is that my lies have been revealed, and there are going to be serious repercussions from that.

I'm not sure whether it is the police that I have to worry about or just the revenge of an angry couple whose marriage I tried to tear apart, but either way, I'm not planning on hanging around long enough to find out. Since hanging up on Ally, I have thrown all my important possessions into a suitcase before throwing everything else into black bags and disposing of it all in the bins outside my flat. Now I am in a taxi headed to the airport with my passport in my handbag, and I plan on taking the first flight out of here. I don't care where I go. I just need to get away because there are going to be some angry people looking for me, and some of them might want to hurt me.

I've committed various offences over the years, both moral and legal, and it remains to be seen just how many of them are going to be exposed. But while I can't change anything incriminating that has already come out, I can ensure that I don't add to my woes by admitting to anything else that I have done wrong. That is why I have disposed of my mobile phone too, ensuring that any recording devices or trackers that a private investigator might be using on me should have been taken care of, allowing me to make my escape in good time.

Of all the targets I have had over the years, I had not expected Sam and Rebecca to be the ones to bring me down. Why couldn't they be like all the other couples and just get a divorce? Why did they have to fight back? Ally's message told me that it was Sam who had hired a PI, and while I admire his fighting spirit, I am unsure as to how he and any investigator were able to track me down and uncover my secrets. That unanswered question is going to bug me for a long time, but it can bug me while I am sitting on a beach abroad rather than in a police station in the UK where I am awaiting questioning.

All the homes I broke into. All the lies I told.

All the lives I destroyed.

Business was good while it lasted, and maybe I'll be able to start up again one day in the future, but for now, I have no one to blame for this mess but myself. Maybe I got complacent, or perhaps I was just due some bad luck after getting away with so much for so long. Maybe I was always going to get found out in the end. Whatever has happened in the past, all I can affect now is the immediate future and my immediate future lies overseas.

I can see the lights of the airport terminal up ahead, and I'm impressed with how quickly my taxi driver has gotten me here. He obviously doesn't know that I am potentially running from the law right now, but I appreciate his haste anyway. What I don't appreciate is the fact that it's approaching midnight, and it's unlikely that I am going to be able to get a flight out of here this evening. I will go in and check, but I'm expecting to be told that the next flight will be leaving at dawn, so I might have to make do with a room at the airport hotel for the next few hours. But it's worth a try anyway, and I waste no time in dragging my suitcase out of the back of the taxi and pulling it behind me into the terminal.

My shoes clatter across the marble floor as I approach the desk, but the fact there are no queues anywhere suggests that I am right in thinking that there are no flights taking off from here over the next few hours. The pretty woman behind the desk is polite enough to confirm that information for me, and my eyes watch her lipstick red lips as she tells me about the first available plane seat being on a 06:40 flight to Lisbon tomorrow morning. I tell her that will do and make the necessary booking before enquiring about a room for the night at the nearby hotel. Fortunately, there is some availability, so I make my way back out of the airport and take the shuttle bus that will drop me at the hotel door.

After checking in and reaching my room, it is a relief to close the door and drop my suitcase onto the bed. I'm not a fan of running but it has to be done, and I will keep running until I am sure that I am safe. I underestimated Sam and the lengths he would go to in order to prove his innocence. That was my mistake. But I won't be making any more mistakes. And maybe I won't be knocking on any more front doors again either.

This might be the sign I needed to have a change of career. I got thrown into this life after my experience with Devon, but that doesn't mean that is the best life for me. I could find something else to do. It probably won't pay as well, but it won't hurt as many people either.

I'm just about to start getting undressed before climbing into bed and getting a few hours of shuteye before my early morning flight when I hear the knock on my hotel room door.

I have no idea who it is. I'm not even sure I want to answer it. But just like all those people whose front doors I knocked on over the years, I might not have a choice.

I am going to have to open it.

47

REBECCA

What started with a knock at the door is going to end with one too. I am standing outside this hotel room waiting for the door to open so I can come face to face again with the woman who sent my life into a tailspin not so long ago. This will be the first time I have seen this woman since she came to my house and told me that my husband had cheated on me, and that night, she had all the power. But now it is me who has the upper hand.

I'm the one knocking.

And she will be the one who is sent into a tailspin.

After several seconds have passed without the door being opened, I decide to knock again but much firmer this time.

'Who is it?'

I detect fear in the enquiry from the other side of the door, but that isn't going to stop me. It only makes me knock again.

I take a deep breath as I wait, knowing how important it is to stay calm so that I am able to say what I came here to say when I finally get the chance. I don't have to wait too long after that because I hear the sound of the handle turning, and two seconds later, the door is open.

Alexandra looks afraid, as she might well be, but she also seems a little relieved that I am on my own. She might have been expecting the police or possibly Sam, but instead, she's just got me.

She might think that it will be easier to handle me.

But she would be wrong.

'Nice to see you again,' I say with a straight face. 'I thought it was my turn to come and surprise you.'

'How the hell did you find me?' Alexandra asks as her eyes dart past me and into the corridor beyond, but I keep my gaze firmly on her.

'The same way I found out your name and what you do for a living,' I reply. 'The same way my husband was able to prove to me that he didn't cheat on me and stop me from divorcing him.'

'The private investigator,' Alexandra mutters, and I nod to confirm her answer.

'You've been watched for a while now, so I wouldn't feel too bad about it. Once they knew who you were, you never stood a chance.'

'Look, I'm sorry for what I did, but it wasn't personal. It was just a job.'

'Just a job,' I repeat with a laugh. 'My whole life was just a job, was it?'

'That's not what I mean.'

'Then tell me what you do mean.'

Alexandra looks like she is starting to realise that I might not be an easier touch than my husband would have been if he was here instead.

'You don't know what it's like to love somebody you can't have.'

Alexandra's words catch me off guard a little.

'What are you talking about?'

'I'm talking about people who are lonely and have to spend their lives alone because their dream partner is already taken. I'm talking about your friend, Ally, having to watch you be happy with Sam while she was secretly pining for him.'

'Ally had no right to try and break my marriage apart. And neither did you!'

'You're correct, but what gives you the right to be happier than somebody else just because you got there first?'

'I got there first?'

'Yes, you met Sam before Ally did. But what is to say that he might have been meant for her instead? What is to say that he might have been happier with her over you?'

I'm not entirely sure what I had been expecting to happen when I came here, but one thing I wasn't banking on was Alexandra giving an impassioned defence of my former best friend.

'You're deluded. You and all the people who pay you to do this crazy thing. What you have done is wrong, and you know it.'

'So what do you want from me? An apology? Fine, I'm sorry. But you got your husband back, so it all worked out well in the end. Now, if you don't mind, I need to get some sleep.'

Alexandra goes to close the door on me, but I shoot out a hand to stop her.

'I haven't finished,' I say as I look at her face through the small gap where the door is still open. But Alexandra doesn't want to know what else I came here to say, and she tries to close the door again.

If it was just me then I might have had a problem keeping her from closing it, but fortunately, Sam accompanied me here this evening and he has been lurking around the corner of the door during this conversation, ready to make an appearance if needed. Now he is needed, and he gives me some assistance in pushing back on the door and getting it fully open again, much to Alexandra's dismay.

Then we force our way into the room and close the door behind us.

Alexandra goes for the hotel room phone, presumably to try and call reception and tell them that two people have just entered her room against her will, but Sam pulls the cord from the wall before she can make the call.

'What are you doing? Get away from me!' Alexandra cries, and I'm aware that some of the other guests on this floor might be able to hear all the commotion, so my husband and I better make this quick.

'You have no idea how much I want to hurt you, and I will do unless you sit down on the bed and shut up.'

Sam's command is a stern one, and it's a little disconcerting to hear him talk in that manner, but his words do the job in getting Alexandra to stop making so much noise, and she takes a seat on the bed in front of us.

'This is what is going to happen,' I say, taking over again. 'We have the names of all the couples you did this to, but what we don't have is their addresses or the names of the people who paid you to break them apart. But you're going to give them to us, and you're going to accompany us as we go around and make sure all those people learn the truth about what has really happened.'

'Why would I do that?' Alexandra snarls back at me, but I just smile.

'Because if you don't then the police are going to be getting involved, and I don't think you want that, do you?'

'Tell the police. I don't care. You don't have much evidence.'

'We have plenty, and I have a feeling we have only just started to scratch the surface,' I say as I stand over Alexandra and glare down at her. 'The police might not care about the lies you told, but I think they will be interested in the things you left in people's homes and how you came to be in their homes in the first place.'

'It's just your word against mine.'

'No, it's your word against dozens of other couples who have had their lives ruined by you as well.'

Alexandra takes that on board, and she can see how deadly serious I am about ensuring she gets a criminal conviction if I am forced to go down that route.

'Say I do what you want. How do I know you won't just tell the police anyway?'

'I guess you'll just have to trust me. Just like I trusted you when you came to my door and told me a lie.'

Alexandra has nothing to say to that, and she lowers her head to avoid my stare.

'Just be grateful that neither me or my husband are the kind of people who lose their tempers easily and commit acts of violence against those who have wronged us,' I say. 'Otherwise, you would really be in trouble then.'

With that ominous statement, I tell the room owner that it is time for us to leave her in peace but that she is being watched and that she should not board that flight in the morning if she wants this all to end without the police involved.

Then I follow Sam to the door, and he opens it to allow me out first.

'How did you find me?' Alexandra asks just before we leave, and Sam and I pause in the doorway.

We share a look, and I know we are both deciding whether to tell her about our neighbour's camera and how this mystery all got unravelled from there. That would surely be a source of comfort for Alexandra to know what mistake she had made, but that's exactly why neither of us feels like divulging that information to her. We don't want to give her that closure, nor do we want to give her a heads-up about something she might end up looking out for in the future if she ever does anything like this again. Instead, we just walk through the door and allow it to close behind us, leaving Alexandra alone in that room to think about what she has done and what she is going to do next.

'Do you think she will try and run?' Sam asks me as we walk away down the corridor.

'No, I think she knows what's best for her, and I think she understood that I was telling her the truth about not getting the police involved if she stays,' I say as we reach the lift that will take us back down to the ground floor. 'Because unlike her, I am not a liar.'

I press the button to send for the lift, but before it can get to this floor, Sam takes my hand and turns me around so that I am looking right at him.

'I'm not a liar either,' he tells me and my heart breaks because I know he is right, yet I spent so long believing he had betrayed me.

I already said it when we were standing outside our house earlier this evening, but I will say it again because I feel like I need to.

'I'm so sorry for not trusting you,' I tell him, shaking my head. 'She was just so convincing. She had so many tricks.'

'I know,' Sam says as he pulls me in for a hug and kisses my head. 'But it's over now, and the main thing is that we both know the truth.'

The lift arrives and the door slides open, but neither of us move, instead content to stay in each other's arms for another minute. By the time we do decide to get into the lift, we are both ready to go home and get into bed. It will be the first night we have spent the night sleeping beside each other in a while, although I'm not sure how much sleeping will be getting done. I have some making up to do to my husband, and I'm sure he wants to make me feel better about myself too.

It doesn't take long for the lift to deposit us into the reception area, and Sam and I walk hand in hand across the marble floor towards the exit, nodding at Erica as we go. She is staying here this evening to make sure that Alexandra doesn't vanish again, and she is doing it because we are paying her a bonus to thank her for all that she and her assistant have done for us.

Our marriage was so close to being over. The lies had threatened to ruin us. The woman at the door almost won. But she didn't. Instead, I won. Sam won.

Love won.

But love is a cruel game and not everybody can win, and as I get into the taxi that will take Sam and I back home, I can't help but think of Ally, Alexandra and all the other people in the world who do desperate things in order to find love for themselves or others.

I know that I am lucky to have my husband, and he is lucky to have me. Not everybody is as lucky as us. If they were then Alexandra would never have been able to run a business like she did. That's why the next thought is a troubling one. It's the thought that there might be other people out there like Alexandra now, spreading lies and rumours and threatening to break happy couples apart.

I can't stop them all. I was barely able to stop one.

I just hope they never come calling at your door.

If they do, it's best if you don't answer.

A Letter from the Author

Thank you for reading *The Woman At The Door*. I hope you had as much fun delving into the lives of Rebecca, Sam and Alexandra as I had creating them. I love to write and I hope my story gave you a little entertainment and escapism from the realities of the world.

Without readers like you, I wouldn't be living my dream as a full-time author, so thank you for picking up this book and thank you for any review you may choose to leave for it afterwards. Reviews really are the most powerful way of getting attention for my books as they help bring in new readers. If you have enjoyed this book then I would be extremely grateful if you could spend a couple of minutes leaving an honest review on Amazon or Goodreads (it can be as short as you like).

Thank you and I hope you enjoy your next read.

Daniel

If you would like to get the latest news about my future books, receive free stories and learn more about the life of a writer, you can join my e-mail list at *www.danielhurstbooks.com*

Also By Daniel Hurst

TIL DEATH DO US PART

What if your husband was your worst enemy?

Megan thinks that she has the perfect husband and the perfect life. Craig works all day so that she doesn't have to, leaving her free to relax in their beautiful and secluded country home. But when she starts to long for friends and purpose again, Megan applies for a job in London, much to her husband's disappointment. She thinks he is upset because she is unhappy. But she has no idea.

When Megan secretly attends an interview and meets a recruiter for a drink, Craig decides it is time to act. Locking her away in their home, Megan realises that her husband never had her best interests at heart. Worse, they didn't meet by accident. Craig has been planning it all from the start.

As Megan is kept shut away from the world with only somebody else's diary for company, she starts to uncover the lies, the secrets, and the fact that she isn't actually Craig's first wife after all...

OUT NOW

THE TUTOR

What if you invited danger into your home?

Amy is a loving wife and mother, to her husband Nick, and her two children, Michael and Bella. It's that dedication to her family that causes her to seek help for her teenage son when it becomes apparent that he is going to fail his end of school exams.

Enlisting the help of a professional tutor, Amy is certain that she is doing the best thing for her son, and indeed, her family. But when she discovers that there is more to this tutor than meets the eye, it is already too late.

With the rest of her family enamoured by the tutor, Amy is the only one who can see that there is something not quite right about her. But as the tutor becomes more involved in Amy's family, it's not just the present that is threatened. Secrets from the past are exposed too, and by the time everything is out in the open, Amy isn't just worried about her son and his exams anymore. She is worried for the survival of her entire family.

This will be one lesson they will never forget.

OUT NOW

RUN AWAY WITH ME

What if your partner was wanted by the police?

Laura is feeling content with her life. She is married, she has a good home, and she is due to give birth to her first child any day now. But her perfect world is shattered when her husband comes home flustered and afraid. He's made a terrible mistake. He's done a bad thing. *And now the police are going to be looking for him.*

There's only one way out of this. He wants to run. *But he won't go without his wife…*

Laura knows it is wrong. She knows they should stay and face the music. But she doesn't want to lose her man. She can't raise this baby alone. *So she agrees to go with him.* But life on the run is stressful and unpredictable and as time goes by, Laura worries she has made a terrible mistake. They should never have ran. But it's too late for that now. Her life is ruined. The only question is: *how will it end?*

OUT NOW

THE ROLE MODEL

She raised her. Now she must help her…

Heather is a single mum who has always done what's best for her daughter, Chloe. From childhood up to the age of seventeen, Chloe has been no trouble. That is until one night when she calls her mother with some shocking news.

There's been an accident. *And now there's a dead body…*

As always, Heather puts her daughter's safety before all else, but this might be one time when she goes too far. Instead of calling the emergency services, Heather hides the body, saving her daughter from police interviews and public outcry.

But as she well knows, everything she does has an impact on her child's behaviour, and as time goes on and the pair struggle to keep their sordid secret hidden, Heather begins to think that she hasn't been such a good mum after all.

In fact, she might have been the worst role model ever…

OUT NOW

THE BROKEN VOWS

He broke his word to her. Now she wants revenge...

Alison is happily married to Graham, or at least she is until she finds out that he has been cheating on her. Graham has broken the vows he made on his wedding day. How could he do it? It takes Alison a while to figure it out, but at least she has time on her side. *Only that is where she is wrong.*

A devastating diagnosis means the clock is ticking down on her life now and if she wants revenge on her cheating partner then she is going to have to act fast. Alison does just that, implementing a dangerous and deadly plan, and it's one that will have far reaching consequences for several people, including her clueless husband.

Hell hath no fury like a woman scorned...

OUT NOW

INFLUENCE

Would you kill for a million followers?

Emily Bennett dreams of being a social media influencer, just like her idols, Mason Manor & Ivy Lane. But shortly after Ivy's untimely death she is contacted by a secretive businessman who offers her the chance at the fame and fortune she so desperately craves.

While Emily initially gets to experience the things she has always wanted, it soon becomes clear that her new employer had sinister motives for approaching her and it isn't long before she discovers that the life of her dreams comes with the kind of conditions that are the stuff of nightmares.

Social media isn't life or death.

It's more important than that.

OUT NOW

THE 20 MINUTE SERIES

20 Chapters. 20 Characters. 20 intertwining stories.

An original psychological thriller series showing how we are all more connected to each other than we think.

What readers are saying:

"If you like people watching then you will love these books!"

"The psychological insight was fascinating, the stories were absorbing and the characters were 3D. I absolutely loved it."

"The books in this series are an incredibly easy read, you become invested in the lives of the characters so easily and I am eager to know more and more. Roll on the next book."

THE 20 MINUTES SERIES (in order)

20 MINUTES ON THE TUBE
20 MINUTES LATER
20 MINUTES IN THE PARK
20 MINUTES ON HOLIDAY
20 MINUTES BY THE THAMES
20 MINUTES AT HALLOWEEN
20 MINUTES AROUND THE BONFIRE
20 MINUTES BEFORE CHRISTMAS
20 MINUTES OF VALENTINE'S DAY
20 MINUTES TO CHANGE A LIFE
20 MINUTES IN LAS VEGAS
20 MINUTES IN THE DESERT

About The Author

Daniel Hurst lives in the North West of England with his wife, Harriet, and considers himself extremely fortunate to be able to write stories every day for his readers.

You can visit him at his online home www.danielhurstbooks.com

You can connect with Daniel on Facebook at www.facebook.com/danielhurstbooks or on Instagram at www.instagram.com/danielhurstbooks

He is always happy to receive emails from readers at daniel@danielhurstbooks.com and replies to every single one.

Thank you for reading.

Daniel

Made in United States
North Haven, CT
06 May 2022

18967395R00182